Harry Buxton Forman, Guild of Women Binders

The Books of William Morris

described with some account of his doings in literature and in the allied crafts

Harry Buxton Forman, Guild of Women Binders

The Books of William Morris
described with some account of his doings in literature and in the allied crafts

ISBN/EAN: 9783337367787

Printed in Europe, USA, Canada, Australia, Japan

Cover: Foto ©Andreas Hilbeck / pixelio.de

More available books at **www.hansebooks.com**

THE BOOKS OF
WILLIAM MORRIS

DESCRIBED

WITH SOME ACCOUNT OF HIS DOINGS IN LITERATURE AND IN THE ALLIED CRAFTS

BY

H. BUXTON FORMAN, C.B.,

AUTHOR OF "OUR LIVING POETS," "THE SHELLEY LIBRARY," ETC., AND EDITOR OF THE WORKS OF SHELLEY AND KEATS

LONDON
FRANK HOLLINGS, 7 GREAT TURNSTILE, HOLBORN
1897

DEAR SON,—In this poor gift there's fitness;
  For when into the world you came,
You got—and let this leaf bear witness—
  A twice associated name.

Our well-belov'd friend Bucke's prenomen
  We gave you—and the letters show it :
Still, we'd an eye upon the omen
  That that same name described a poet.

'Tis naught but simple truth I'm telling—
  Two sponsors' names in one we found,
With some slight difference in the spelling
  And none whatever in the sound.

While yet a lad you loved to walk about
  The book-room mingling lore with chaff;
And well you knew some tomes I talk about
  In this my biobibliograph.

Later, the "midnight lamp" has seen us
  In that same book-room all alone ;
But since the Atlantic heaved between us
  Those Morris rows have grown and grown ;

And still with every teeming year
  That made the listening world his debtor
I grew to hold the man more dear
  And ever loved the poet better.

(Ah ! Morris, it was well to know you—
  Whatever comes of it, it *was* well—
Though dry the sprigs of bay I throw you,
  Right fain were I to be your Boswell !)

So long, dear Boy ! The ship's in port
  That scores the Atlantic east and west ;
Those rollers huge she'll make her sport,
  And bring you this at my behest.

CONTENTS.

ILLUSTRATIONS.

PREFACE.

THE objects of the present work may be stated in few words. Convinced that "the world of books is still," of all worlds in which an artist is privileged to live, the most "living world," I have thought that a true presentment of the man would be the natural result of setting forth in a connected narrative the public appearances of Morris in literature, from the time when, as an undergraduate, he founded and maintained THE OXFORD AND CAMBRIDGE MAGAZINE, to the quite recent date on which his trustees issued the last but one of the posthumous writings destined to come from his Kelmscott Press. It is a great record as well as a long one. It is one in connexion with which the student and collector of this latter end of the nineteenth century is entitled to look for exact bibliographical knowledge; and I have tried to weave that knowledge into the thread of the narrative in such a manner as to present, with the aid of typographical arrangements and some pictorial illustration, a true portraiture of each book, and always with the hope that somewhere in the vicinity of such portraiture there will be something written or depicted to conjure up in the reader's eye at least the shadowy image of the man who lives in each and all of Morris's many books.

With that aim, it seemed best to begin by giving a summary appreciation of the facts of his public life. Apart from his doings in literature, which it is the main purpose of the

*following pages to record and illustrate, the epochs of his life are
so many important chapters in the history of arts and crafts in
England, and in the social and political movement which is still
going on for the benefit of the handicraftsman. It will not be for
me to deal at large with the period when he started his business
undertaking on æsthetic grounds to reform our views of colour,
curve, line, texture—in a word, our tastes—or to show how this
threw him into those relations with handicraftsmen which could
lead his generous heart but one way—to make the handicraftsman's life joyful, as his was joyful; for what man ever so joyed,
so revelled, in twenty different methods of work as William
Morris did? Others will doubtless tell how, in developing his
views for the workmen, he enlarged his scope; how from import-
ing rough but comely pottery out of France, he got to influencing
the manufacture and securing the distribution of de Morgan lustre
—a lost art revived; how from bringing home Eastern carpets
he grew to see that, after all, these were not the fittest and best
for our Western civilization, and how he set up his dye-works
and looms and made fabrics and carpets which will influence the
taste of the Western world when he has been dead a century.
More important still will be the history of how he entered into
the practical side of the Socialist propaganda and went on
fearlessly till convinced, not that he would come to harm—for he
had always all to lose and nothing to gain—but that "ructions
with police," as he phrased it, would injure the cause. And
history will have to tell sooner or later the tale of his seeing
what a base, mechanical thing was become this great art of
printing of ours, and of his setting up the Kelmscott Press, to
issue books in which every letter should be beautiful. But I
cannot help recalling here that, just as his friends and dependents
were laying him to rest in the quiet little Oxfordshire village
which gives that press its name, the fortunate possessors of the
great folio Chaucer edited by his old friend Frederick Ellis and
beautified by the stately and profoundly sympathetic pictures of*

his older friend Sir Edward Burne-Jones, were turning in wonder the pages of one of the noblest books ever printed. It is some satisfaction to remember that the brave man and great artist who crammed the joyous labour of three life-times into sixty-two years and a half, taking the rough with the smooth to benefit his humbler fellow-craftsmen, saw with his eyes this crowning work of many applied arts and crafts before he entered into his rest.

For much information cheerfully supplied, for drawings or blocks lent for purposes of illustration, for permission to use copyright designs or works, my thanks are due to many friends and correspondents. Without attempting to allocate each particular obligation, I will record my gratitude to Mrs. Sparling, Mr. Frederick S. Ellis, Mr. Sidney Cockerell, Mr. Walter Crane, Mr. Emery Walker, Dr. Richard Garnett, Canon R. W. Dixon, Judge Lushington, Mr. Clement Shorter, Mr. Thomas J. Wise, Mr. F. Hollyer, Mr. William Reeves, Mr. G. B. Shaw, Mr. H. M. Hyndman, Mr. Edward Bell, Mr. A. H. Bullen, Mr. Gilbert Ellis, Mr. Walter A. Brook, Messrs. Roberts Brothers of Boston, Mass., and the Proprietors of the Chiswick Press. I feel that this imperfect list does not include all of those who have kindly answered letters about details dealt with in the following pages; and I beg that all, whether named or unnamed, will accept my cordial thanks.

H. BUXTON FORMAN.

46, Marlborough Hill, St. John's Wood,
   31 October 1897.

INTRODUCTION

THE LIFE POETIC AS LIVED BY
WILLIAM MORRIS

INTRODUCTION.

The Life Poetic as lived by William Morris.

IT was at Walthamstow in Essex, on the 24th of March 1834, that the Welsh child destined to become the great artist and reformer whose doings are the subject of this book first saw the light. His father was a London merchant, who by fortunate investments became wealthy; and to him it may be that William Morris was indebted for that capacity for affairs which he somehow had, whether born in the blood or not. How his early years were passed it is for other hands to record in due time and with due authority. It is said that he enjoyed great freedom as a boy, had the run of Epping Forest and grew to love it, and rode about the country on his pony, following up a constant quest for old churches—for already the love of architecture was strong in him—and mixing freely with stablemen and others of like rank, from whom he probably learnt a great deal more good than harm. He did not attach much importance to his schooling; but certain it is that Marlborough and Oxford (Exeter College) have the honour of his conventional training. It was at Oxford that he got to know his future partner, Faulkner, and Burne-Jones, through whom, later, he became acquainted with Dante Gabriel Rossetti. But he must have been getting his special mental education in his own way long before he left Oxford, for *The Oxford and Cambridge Magazine*, published monthly during the year 1856, teems with work from his "prentice hand," saturated with medievalism. It was also in 1856 that he was articled to the late George Edmund Street, the renowned architect: his early sympathies with what is noblest in architecture may be traced in his remarkable literary work of this period, preserved in the periodical already named, in which he was associated with

1—2

several brilliant young contemporaries. *The Oxford and Cambridge Magazine* is credibly stated to have been practically founded, and supported so far as funds are concerned, by Morris, although it was not he, but Mr. Fulford, who edited it. It contains poems by Morris, critical papers, and a series of notable prose stories. It is in some of these that he showed, in a dreamy and sensitive way, that keen sympathy with the craftsmen of the Middle Ages which in later years led him into the eager polemics of that practical undertaking the Society for the Protection of Ancient Buildings—dreaded, though never sufficiently dreaded, by the destructive Philistine. Those early stories, though crude in form, bear unmistakable marks of genius; and no man of judgment reading them as the work of a youth of one or two and twenty could hesitate to predict for that youth a literary career of no ordinary kind. But if these romantic tales, one of which is so recklessly fanciful as to make a dead man the chronicler of his own experiences, were sound material for prophesying good concerning Morris, still more so was his first volume of poetry, *The Defence of Guenevere and other Poems*, issued in 1858. This, by the way, includes the little privately printed *Sir Galahad*, figuring between the magazine and the book in the chronological account further on. In the whole volume the life of our medieval ancestors is depicted with a sympathetic insight perhaps unparalleled. The reading of Malory and Froissart has stirred to its depths a receptive artist-nature of the rarest kind; and a strength of hand equal to that receptiveness has produced at the age of twenty-four work that must stand or fall with English literature. *Sir Peter Harpdon's End*, *The Haystack in the Floods*, *Shameful Death*, and other pieces in the volume, would be known anywhere as the work of a master. Some poems in the book are immature in craftsmanship; but not one shows defective intuition.

Morris did not remain with Street for the full term of his articles, but made a practical start in a less restricted line than that of architecture. Before he had established himself in literature with the public as distinguished from the few "who know," he had taken the leading part in founding an undertaking then deemed to be somewhat quixotic, but none the less destined to be an important factor in the developement of English taste. It was the author of *The Defence of Guenevere* whose name figured in the style of the firm of fine-art decorators, Morris, Marshall, Faulkner and Co., who began more than a quarter of a century ago an attempt to reform English taste, and make people furnish and decorate their abodes with things beautiful instead of things hideous. This enterprise, in which the late Dante Gabriel Rossetti, the late Ford Madox Brown, and Sir Edward Burne-Jones were associated, was ultimately and up to Morris's death, conducted under his name only, with the simplified commercial style of " Morris and Co." It may fairly claim the principal place among the agencies which have brought about a great and favourable change in the style of our domestic decoration and in our taste for colour. The so-called æsthetic movement was a mere bastard off-shoot of this genuine reform; but the reform itself is still going on steadily, notwithstanding the transient reflected ridicule which it incurred through the *gauche* eccentricities of its by-blow. Those who remember the arrival from Paris of the fine colours (since nicknamed " æsthetic "), which superseded in women's attire the crude horrors affected by the last generation, 'may be pleased to doubt the credit given above to Morris in this matter. Nevertheless, the truth is that the French milliners, who sent those colours hither to our women, got them from Morris's upholstery stuffs.

The year 1867 must be set down as that in which Morris established himself with the public as a poet who had mastered the tale-teller's craft. In that year appeared *The Life and Death of Jason*, a narrative poem in seventeen books, written in five-foot iambic couplets of the Chaucerian model, as distinguished from the Waller-Dryden-Pope distich. Indeed, Chaucer was the acknowledged master of Morris at this time, and is recalled to the reader's recollection in the next work, *The Earthly Paradise*, of which the first instalment appeared in 1868, and the last in 1870. In that treasure-house of lovely tales and lyric interludes, distinguished by their manliness and sincerity from the introspective mosaics of the day, the stock metres, three in number, derive from Chaucer, while the tales themselves are of various origin—mainly Greek or Northern, but drawn occasionally, either directly or indirectly, from the East. While *The Earthly Paradise* was in progress, Morris was becoming deep in Icelandic literature. From this he not only derived the magnificent tragic story of *The Lovers of Gudrun*, in which *The Earthly Paradise* sounds its deepest notes, and soars highest, but he also enriched our literature with prose versions of several of the sagas, being assisted by Mr. Eiríkr Magnússon. *The Story of Grettir the Strong*, published in 1869, represents the ruder domestic sagas of the tenth century. *The Story of the Volsungs and Niblungs*, issued in the following year, represents the primeval mythic literature of the race. The two shorter sagas of *Frithiof the Bold* and *Gunnlaug the Wormtongue* are admirable samples of Icelandic legend and domestic romance : the translations of them were executed near about the same period as the two large works, and appeared in periodicals. All these works are interspersed with snatches of scaldic song in the alliterative measures of the Icelanders ; and with the version of *Völsunga* Morris gave a considerable number of the songs of the *Elder Edda*.

In literature, as in life and its varied pursuits, his work divides itself into definite periods, of which the chronological minutiæ will be found in their place. Considered in the light of a poet and story-teller, he may be said to have started on his career as an Anglo-Norman medievalist, drawing, however, considerable inspiration from the Greek and Latin classics, and gradually, with a widening area of knowledge and reading, taking in at first hand influences from the sturdy literature of the Northmen who peopled Iceland. From the pure medievalism of *The Defence of Guenevere, Sir Peter Harpdon's End, The Haystack in the Floods*, and the Chaucerian classicism of *The Life and Death of Jason*, we pass through *The Earthly Paradise* to find the flavour far more Northern at the end than at the beginning ; the actual work of translating large Icelandic sagas had effected a great change, and had led to the transformation of one Icelandic prose masterpiece, *The Saga of the Laxdale Men*, into that poetic masterpiece *The Lovers of Gudrun*, which must be regarded as the high-water mark of his first period.

To the second period belong *Love is Enough*, a dramatic and lyric morality, deriving the more marked features of its poetic method from the Icelandic, and also several renderings of Icelandic sagas, though some of them remained in manuscript till a recent date. The period is that in which Morris shows, not a mere tincture, but a prevailing feeling of Northern hardiness, has abandoned the three Chaucerian stock metres, and developed a metric system with anapæstic movement surpassing in every vital particular all that has been done in anapæstic measures since Tennyson showed the way in *Maud*.

Love is Enough ; or, the Freeing of Pharamond : a Morality, published in 1873, was the first independent original fruit borne by his revelling in the forthright, simple, manly, and most craftsmanlike narratives of the hardy Norsemen who peopled Iceland. Here Morris employed alliterative metre in a truly masterly manner for the shaping of one of the most noteworthy poems of the third quarter of the century. Though something above the heads of the large public to which *The Earthly Paradise* appeals, it widened the poet's credit with the critical few. Two years later the sagas of Frithiof and Gunnlaug were reprinted, with that of Viglund the Fair, and some shorter Icelandic tales, under the title of *Three Northern Love Stories*, etc. In 1876 Morris issued *The Æneids of Virgil done into English Verse*. The verse chosen was the ballad metre employed by Chapman in translating the Iliad. If the service of the modern poet to Virgil is not in all respects better than that of the Elizabethan to Homer, this latter-day Æneid is at least of a more equable quality, of a finer taste in language, and much more literal than Chapman's Iliad. It is a translation, not a mere paraphrase ; and the metre is handled in the noblest manner. A single sample, the opening of Book X, must illustrate :

> " Meanwhile is opened wide the door of dread Olympus' walls,
> And there the sire of Gods and Men unto the council calls,
> Amid the starry place, wherefrom, high-throned he looks adown
> Upon the folk of Latin land and that beleaguered town."

There is a fidelity to the original here which we seek in vain in such charming couplets of Chapman as these from the opening of Book VIII :

> " The cheerful lady of the light, deck'd in her saffron robe,
> Dispersed her beams through every part of this enflowered globe,
> When thundering Jove a court of Gods assembled by his will,
> In top of all the topful heights, that crown th' Olympian hill,"—

which can hardly be held to render closely what is literally translated thus by Messrs. Lang, Leaf and Myers :

" Now Dawn the saffron-robed was spreading over all the earth, and Zeus whose joy is in the thunder let call an assembly of the gods upon the topmost peak of many-ridged Olympus."

Up to this point Morris might almost be said to have been frankly medieval in his way of looking at things. His spiritual birth into his own century is to be found recorded in his next substantive work, *The Story of Sigurd the Volsung, and the Fall of the Niblungs*, published in 1877. Here not only does he fill a large canvas with an art higher and subtler than that shown in *Jason*, or even in *The Earthly Paradise*, but he betrays a profound concern in the destinies of the race, such as we do not exact from the mere story-teller. Love and adventure he had already treated in a manner approaching perfection; and a sympathetic intelligence of all beautiful legends breathes throughout his works; but Sigurd is something more than a lover and a warrior : he is at once heroic and tragic ; and he is surrounded by characters heroic and tragic. In his mythic person large spiritual questions are suggested ; he is the typical saviour as conceived by the Northern race; and this side of the conception is more emphatic and unmistakable in the modern work than in the *Völsunga Saga*, which is the basis of this great poem. In structure, in metre, and in the adoption of the Icelandic system of imagery into our tongue, *Sigurd the Volsung* is superb. But the genius of the poet is still more evident in the convincingly right conception of all the characters and of the tragic import of their relations one to another—perhaps more than all in the unflinching truth to the savage primeval conception of the incestuous Signy. The real Signy stands in splendid and immortal contrast with her debased counterpart Sieglinde in Wagner's great poem *Der Ring des Nibelungen*. The crime of Sieglinde is self-seeking, and that of her brother Siegmund conscious ; the crime of the real Signy is swallowed up in the tremendous self-renunciation of which it is a part, and the crime of the real Sigmund is unconscious. It is to the unerring rectitude and absolute sanity of Morris's genius that we owe the good hap of this strict adherence to the original mythos in these particulars.

In dealing as none but a modern could have dealt with the greatest myth of our Northern race, Morris, perhaps unconsciously, celebrated what has been called above his spiritual birth into his own century. "Dreamer of dreams, born out of my due time," was never a wholly true description ; but, from the time of Sigurd's "coming into the tale" of the poet's life, his renunciation of the attempt to "set the crooked straight" became specifically inapt. Commencing with an art-propaganda which aimed at the reform of the decorative arts, he gradually slid into social questions of the deepest concern to all men, learned and unlearned. He found the cause of artistic degradation in the rotten commercial foundations of our whole social scheme ; and from that time forth his efforts have tended towards root and branch social reform.

Let it be clearly understood that *Sigurd the Volsung* is no mere rhythmic and metrical triumph, though in those matters its merits are, as has been said, of a superb kind. In the much higher qualities, which derive from knowledge of life, feeling for national myth, epic action and tragic intensity combined, this epic in anapæstic couplets which rounds the second period, stands among the foremost poems not only of this century but of our literature.

The third period, from 1878 to 1890, is chiefly an epoch of lectures, pamphlets, leaflets, and periodical press work (all with a definite social and political object) ; but the literary artist, never quite dormant, gradually gets the upper hand again. It is needless to criticize a series of social and political tracts and articles of which many would be ephemeral but for their authorship. In 1878 Morris issued *The Decorative Arts ; their Relations to Modern Life and Progress, an Address,* and in 1879 a presidential address to the Birmingham Society of Arts; *Labour and Pleasure versus Labour and Sorrow* (a second presidential address) followed in 1880 ; and a reprint of these three, with two other lectures, under the general title *Hopes and Fears for Art,* came out in 1882, *Art and Socialism, a Lecture,* as well as an introduction to Sketchley's *Review of European Society* and *A Summary of the Principles of Socialism written for the Democratic Federation* (conjointly with Mr. H. M. Hyndman), in 1884. *Chants for Socialists,* in several forms, *The Manifesto of the Socialist League, For Whom shall we Vote ?* and *Useful Work versus Useless Toil* belong to 1885. *The Labour Question from the Socialist Standpoint, A Short Account of the Commune of Paris,* written conjointly with E. Belfort Bax and Victor Dave, and *Socialism, a Lecture,* came out in 1886 ; *The Tables Turned ; or, Nupkins Awakened : a Socialist Interlude,* as for the *First Time Played at the Hall of the Socialist League on*

Saturday, October 15*th*, 1887, was published the same year as a pamphlet; and so were *The Aims of Art* and *A Death Song* (for Alfred Linnell, killed in Trafalgar Square, November 20, 1887). This record of bare facts for the year in question would be incomplete without a mention of *The Commonweal*, the organ of the Socialist League, established under Morris's editorship and with his financial support at the beginning of 1885, as a monthly sheet, but carried on as a weekly news-paper from May-Day 1886 until after he gave up the editor-ship in 1890. The pages of this print teem with Morris's manly and outspoken attacks on commercialism — attacks delivered in a cause from the success of which he has per-sonally all to lose and nothing to gain. There are also in *The Commonweal* many productions of his pen that are anything but ephemeral. From the list of pamphlets must be taken, as of special and independent literary interest, apart from the Socialist propaganda, *Chants for Socialists*, *The Tables Turned*, and the *Death Song ;* but a far higher effort than these is the poem of modern life called *The Pilgrims of Hope*, which lies buried in the first two volumes of *The Commonweal*. That poem, written in the great manner of *Sigurd the Volsung*, and mainly in the same metre, is ostensibly a complete treatment of a modern Socialist subject, and runs to over 1,300 lines. Although this was privately reprinted, the poet has kept it by him to render it more perfect in form ; but whether he has left any revision or not, the poem will ultimately rank among his leading works, and is likely to remain, for another generation of English readers, the most remarkable thing in the distinctly militant literature of the Socialist movement among us.

The Odyssey of Homer done into English Verse, put forth in 1887, was something of an astonishment for those who knew of the various claims on the poet's time and energy. It is as literal as his version of the *Æneid*, and even finer in metric qualities, the verse being, not the ballad metre of the Virgil, but once more the anapæstic couplet of *Sigurd the Volsung*, which Morris has made peculiarly his own. It may be doubted whether these renderings of Virgil and Homer do not stand alone as being at once faithful to the sense of the originals, and poetic literature of the highest class. In the following year (1888) he issued a further Socialist pamphlet, *True and False Society*, and accomplished a very novel piece of purely literary propagandism under the title *A Dream of John Ball;* the poet in a dream sees something of Jack Straw's rebellion, and discusses at large with the revolutionary ecclesiastic of that period, John Ball, the future of labour in England, culminating in the effacement of genuine handicraft by machinery under the commercial system. This noble prose work, which first appeared from week to week in *The Commonweal*, was reprinted as a book, with a story of kindred interest called *A King's Lesson*, in 1888. In the same year the poet took an active part in the establishment of the Arts and Crafts Exhibition Society, in whose catalogues there are technical essays from his pen; and he published, under the general title *Signs of Change*, a collection of his social and artistic lectures, old and new.

The year 1889 had a fresh surprise in store, to wit, a wholly new thing in English prose fiction, *A Tale of the House of the Wolfings and all the Kindreds of the Mark, written in prose and in verse by William Morris*, a wonderful myth-romance of the tribal period of the Goths. The Mark is the name given to a series of clearings in a vast forest, peopled by certain tribes of Goths. Neither period nor place is specified. Perhaps it will be safe to regard the dealings of the Goths and Romans here depicted as proper to the fourth century, the historical event of which a reflexion in small may be detected, being the overthrow of the Romans under Valens by the Goths; and, as Mirkwood water, the river running through the Mark, flows northward, it may perhaps be regarded as some feeder of the Danube. In dealing with this early period, it is fitting that myth should mingle with matter-of-fact. The secret union of the hero Thiodolf, the head of the House of the Wolfings, with a daughter of Odin, a Chooser of the Slain, by name the Wood-Sun, is treated with rare dignity; and their daughter the Hall-Sun, the virgin guardian of the sacred lamp of that name which hangs in the Wolfing Hall, is a character of heroic mould. The material part of the story is an attempt of a large body of Romans to possess themselves of the Mark, and their overthrow and annihilation by the Markmen: the romantic motive running through the book is a hauberk myth nobler in conception even than the hauberk myth of " the golden Sigurd," who so often for reasons good in his dealings with the varied evils that infest the earth

" Did on the Helm of Aweing, and the Hauberk all of gold,
    Whose like is not in the heavens, nor has earth of its fellow told."

The hauberk bestowed by the Wood-Sun upon Thiodolf, with
a lying assurance that no " evil weird " hung to it, was got by
fraud from a dwarf, whose curse it bore, together with its own
unchangeable virtue. That curse was that, though the shirt of
mail should save the wearer, it should wreck his folk ; and it is
Thiodolf's great renunciation of the hauberk, and with it of the
Wood-Sun and life, that gives to his death in his people's
victory the quality of a sorrow swallowed up in splendour ;
while the devoted isolation of the Hall-Sun, whose influence
brings all this to pass, makes her continuance in life more
tragic than her father's death. The book has little in common
with anything more modern than the great Icelandic sagas,
most of which it excels in grandeur of conception, in beauty of
form, and in subtlety of transition from prose to verse. The
metrical passages in which the book abounds are reserved for
the more exalted and emotional phases of the dialogue, and
reach the highest level of *Sigurd the Volsung*.

This great work was followed late in the same year by *The
Roots of the Mountains, wherein is told somewhat of the Lives
of the Men of Burgdale, their Friends, their Neighbours, their
Foemen and their Fellows-in-Arms*. The subject is akin to
that of *The House of the Wolfings* ; but the period is consider-
ably later, the Goths having passed from the tribal state to
that of village communities, though retaining some of the noble
primitive institutions of the tribal state as described by the
poet. Here again the motive is defence of the land against
invasion ; but in this case the " dusky men," whom the Burg-
dalers combine with a remnant of the Wolfings to overthrow,
may be taken to be of Hunnish race.   Their anti-human
institutions leave but little room for horror at their extermina-
tion like vermin. In laying out, *The Roots of the Mountains*
is no whit inferior to *The House of the Wolfings*. There are
those who award it the higher place. It is, however, naturally
of a less exalted poetical pitch, the epoch being too late for fact
longer to mingle with myth. On the other hand, there is the
compensating advantage of a very human love-motive treated
with perfect sympathy and masculine vigour, while the numerous
characters are the more lifelike for their less remoteness. For
consistency of delineation these men and women leave nothing

to desire; for realization of place, personality, costume, and institution, the work is unsurpassed ; and in the one matter which in this case is very important, the invention of battle incident, Homer himself could not afford to give the modern poet points.

In 1890 he published a Socialist pamphlet called *Monopoly , or, How Labour is Robbed*, and, in *The English Illustrated Magazine*, another prose romance of a legendary character, *The Glittering Plain; or, the Land of Living Men.* Though characterized by all the force of handling of Morris's later years, this piece, by treating of the renewal of youth without death, as a thing actually accomplished in the tale, recalls to the mind the dreamy period of his own poetic youth.

During the closing months of *The Commonweal* its pages were distinguished by the appearance from week to week of *News from Nowhere ; or, an Epoch of Rest, being some Chapters from a Utopian Romance,* in which Morris showed how an artist could deal with a theme cognate to that of Mr. Bellamy's dreary *Looking Backward.* What Morris gives us is a picture of English society as it might be after the socialist revolution to which the propaganda tends. The account given by an antiquary of the way in which the revolution came about is admirable ; but finer still is the description of the renovated Thames country from Hammersmith to Kelmscott ; and perhaps most precious of all the portrait of the ideal woman Ellen, who joins the poet and his companions on the dream-journey at Runnymede, and fades so cruelly out of our sight with the rest of the splendid vision when he awakes in " dingy Hammersmith," and realizes that he has dreamed.

The partial submergence beneath the thick waters of militant socialism was now drawing to a close. At no time had the submergence been complete. In *The Tables Turned,* familiarly called " Nupkins," art had suffered most at the hands of doctrine (for *Nupkins* is in its way a work of art); but *The Pilgrims of Hope, A Dream of John Ball,* and *News from Nowhere,* are before all things works of art, though saturated with socialist conviction : they are as distinctly creative as his earlier and later work, though of a more mingled web. With the disruption of the Socialist League and the abandonment of *The Commonweal,* a more hopeful period for art production began, though in a quiet way, at Hammersmith : the poet still presided over the Hammersmith Socialist Society, leaving those who believed in "ructions with the police" to seek amusement of that kind at their own sweet will.

In 1891, in conjunction with Mr. Magnússon, he entered upon a great undertaking in the way of translation from the Icelandic,—*The Saga Library*, of which five volumes have appeared. The first contains three sagas, *The Story of Howard the Halt*, *The Story of the Banded Men*, and *The Story of Hen Thorir*; the second consists of the *Eyrbyggja Saga* with the *Saga of the Heath-Slayings* as an Appendix; and the others are occupied by the *Hemiskringla* of Snorri Sturluson. The rest of the great Icelandic Sagas were to have followed if death had not cut the labour short.

In this same year 1891 came another surprise. Morris had long chafed under the inadequacy of modern printing to the demands of his exacting artistic taste. He determined to set up printing works of his own; and the renowned Kelmscott Press was the result. Here, of course, he went to work in his customary manner, found out all he could about the history and the ways and means of the craft, got most useful help and counsel from his friend Mr. Emery Walker, and very soon set to work. Not only did he design the beautiful ornamental initial letters and borders used at the Kelmscott Press; he also drew on a large scale every letter in each of the three founts, the Golden type, the Troy type, and the Chaucer type; and, more than this, he drew and redrew until he got each letter perfect and a fit model from which to cut a steel punch, with due intervention of the photographer to reduce his drawings to the right size. He had his own hand-made paper made from pure linen rag, set up hand-presses, obtained the best of ink, employed the best labour he could get, and set good binders to put his sheets together in seemly vellum or parchment; and he issued a great series of masterpieces in the art of printing. Many of his own fourth-period books appeared first in this sumptuous form.

The first task completed at the new press was to give permanent book form to *The Glittering Plain*. This work was reprinted from the numbers of *The English Illustrated Magazine* for June, July, August, and September, 1890; and by the 4th of April 1891, the printing was finished, though it was not till the 8th of May that subscribers received their copies of the

This is the Golden type.

This is the Troy type.

This is the Chaucer type.

Design for letter "h" of the Golden type:
Specimens of the three Kelmscott founts; and
Book-mark used in the smaller volumes.

The larger Book-mark used in the Beowulf and other large Kelmscott volumes.

quaint old-world-looking vellum-bound book, with its chamois leather strings to tie in front and prevent it from opening like an oyster, as vellum-bound books will if given their wicked way.

By the 24th of September 1891, Morris had finished printing his *Poems by the Way*, one of the most striking volumes of short poems issued during the last decade, and thoroughly worthy of the genius of its author. This also was first printed at the Kelmscott Press. The volume includes poems then recently written, as that truly great ballad *The Burghers' Battle* and the deliciously breezy *Goldilocks and Goldilocks*, and some written many years earlier, as *The God of the Poor*. Some had, like that, appeared in periodicals; but none save a piece from *Jason* and a snatch from *The Earthly Paradise* had been in any of Morris's previous books, while by far the greater part had not appeared before at all.

Steady progress was now made at the Press with the re-printing of Morris's own works in the sumptuous and fitting form which he had devised; and this work was accompanied by that of printing or reprinting other books, ancient and modern, deemed worthy of the honour. The next original romance, *The Wood beyond the World*, appeared in the same 8vo. form as *The Glittering Plain* and *Poems by the Way*, but with the addition of a very noble frontispiece by Sir Edward Burne-Jones, representing that lovely creation "the Maid"— Morris's heroine—in her plain white garment, or to use her own words, in her "scanty coat and bare arms and naked feet," with the chaplet, girdle, arm-rings and "sandals" of living meadow flowers which perform so important a part in the story in getting the hero and heroine through perilous lands inhabited by fierce and strange tribes; for had not the maid the magic power to revive the flowers with a touch of her hand?

This work was through the press by May 1894; by January 1895, a translation of *Beowulf*, done in conjunction with the Rev. A. T. Wyatt, had been printed in the Troy type on paper of the size called large quarto at the Kelmscott Press, but ranging very well with seventeenth century folios. It is a most vigorous and virile production, but can scarcely become popular, being more than ordinarily remote from modern feeling.

In *Child Christopher and Goldilind the Fair* Morris got back to a thoroughly human story racy of British earth in the old days,—the story admirably conceived and laid out and the characters drawn with the consistency and vigour to be expected from the liberal hand which had given us Thiodolf and the Hall-Sun, Otter and Arinbjorn, Face-of-God and Bow-May, Hallblithe and the Puny Fox, and all the gallery of living beings whom we meet in *The House of the Wolfings*, *The Roots of the Mountains*, and *The Glittering Plain*. Oakenrealm is the suggestive name of Christopher's country, and Jack of the Tofts that of the grand outlaw who in the end helps him to come to his own: the mere names of these latter books are exhilarating.

But the most considerable of all these romances is *The Well at the World's End*, which was proportionately long at press, and was not completely printed till March 1896. It is a fountain-of-youth story of the most striking and enthralling kind, filling a large quarto volume of 496 pages, printed in double columns in the Chaucer type, full of stir and varied adventure, and dealing but sparely with the supernatural. The murder of the woman, who may be called the Ayesha or "She" of this book, leaves a wound only comparable, for "the pity of it," to that most piteous destruction of the blithe spirit of the Count of Monte Beni, wrought by the unflinching hand of Hawthorne in *The Marble Faun*. Like that tragic act, the murder of the woman who has drunk of the well, and dominates the lives of all men with whom she comes in contact, is an artistic necessity—albeit it comes upon us with a rueful shock—for not until she goes out of the tale can the true, deep-down, human interest of the fable be wrought up to the top of the artist's bent.

Yet two more of these strange and lovely books did the master write before the end, *The Water of the Wondrous Isles* and *The Sundering Flood*; and both will have been delivered from the Kelmscott Press before the year 1897 closes upon us.

These latter romances, together with several volumes of translations from medieval French tales, etc., form a mass of high-class work in all the original part of which Morris showed a strong grip of character and intimate knowledge of the doings of men and communities in various ages. Altogether, counting *John Ball*, here are nine works of fiction in which this master of all the leading crafts that can be named has devised a new method and a fresh form of speech, has laid out his stories with admirable clearness, filled their fabric with beautiful legends, or visions of what has been and what may be, and created a living gallery of men and women, all unmistakable in the differentia of their characters and personalities. If there were no first, second, and third periods at all, these books of his fourth and, alas ! final period would alone suffice to secure him a place among the greatest literary artists of the age and, indeed, of the world.

It is in no formal or conventional sense that I have written "alas !" For to me one of the keenest interests in life was the perennial question, What will William Morris do next? That I was privileged to know him in the flesh for some eight or nine and twenty years added a zest to that interest. As he said to his friend and colleague Hyndman, the world was a jolly world to him, and he had plenty to do still. During the last years of fruitful work, while he was writing those prose tales, designing letters and borders for his press, looking specially after the sumptuous Chaucer with its illustrations by Sir Edward Burne-Jones, presiding over the business side of his undertakings, lecturing and influencing by other means various movements, philanthropic in the highest sense, and following up with a boyish eagerness the formation of that astonishing collection of medieval books and manuscripts of which the world has heard so much,—while all this was going on, the footstep of death, though unheard, was hard upon the threshold of his door. Hopes were entertained that a sea-trip to the North would help him through some of the physical disabilities which had come upon him ; but here there was disappointment. As Mr. Hyndman has recorded, he did not disguise from his friends the irksomeness of his illness. "If," said he, "it merely means that I am to be laid up for a little while, it doesn't so much matter, you know ; but if I am to be caged up here for months, and then it is to be the end of all things, I shouldn't like it at all. This has been a jolly world to me, and I find plenty to do in it."

Plenty indeed ! And how full it all is of the "beauty of the skin" of that "jolly world," how rich and racy of the soil of that noble and generous heart ! But it *was* to be "the end of all things"; and on the 3rd of October 1896 William Morris passed peacefully away at Kelmscott House in the Upper Mall, Hammersmith.

With all its extraordinary variety his life, if looked at with a philosophic eye, or even with an eye of moderate sagacity, presents a beautiful unity. Speaking of literature alone, it is not too much to say that the boyish romances in *The Oxford and Cambridge Magazine* are the lineal ancestors of the great works which poured from the Kelmscott Press. These last have the same superlative merit as his other mature works whether in verse or in prose. He always saw things with absolute clearness, and had power to make others see them also. In a large proportion of his work the wider life of old times drew his gaze irresistibly; and the contemplation made him somewhat sorrowful. After he had mixed for many years in the affairs of modern life, and had realized more than ever the awful contrast between misery and happiness, Hope " came into the tale "; and reasonable hope begets tenfold desire. His latter books depict states of society in which happiness is possible to every man, even though the happiness be but that of dying for the general good. The worst his enemies could say of him at last was that he had passed from one beautiful dream to another—from a dream of the golden mythical past to a dream of the golden possible future.

BEGINNINGS

THE OXFORD AND CAMBRIDGE MAGAZINE
SIR GALAHAD—A CHRISTMAS MYSTERY
THE DEFENCE OF GUENEVERE AND OTHER POEMS

2—2

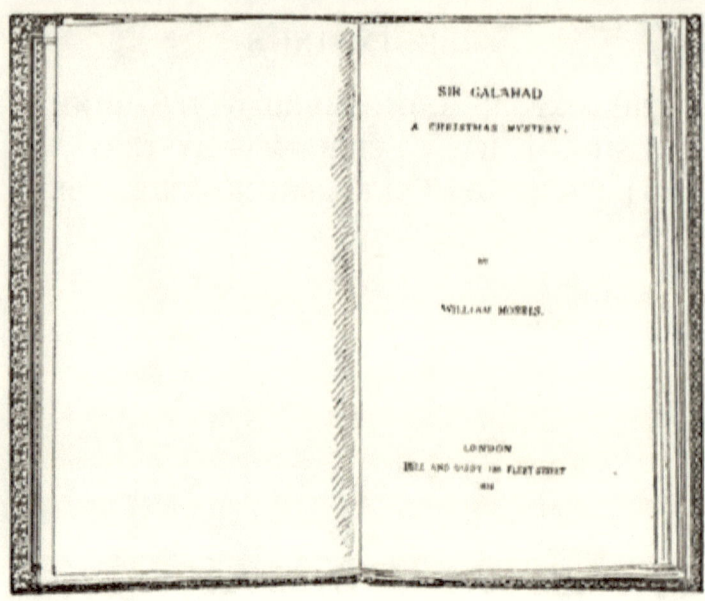

SIR GALAHAD, A CHRISTMAS MYSTERY, BOUND IN MOROCCO BY RIVIÈRE.

BEGINNINGS :

THE OXFORD AND CAMBRIDGE MAGAZINE—SIR GALAHAD, A
CHRISTMAS MYSTERY—THE DEFENCE OF GUENEVERE
AND OTHER POEMS.

NOT very long ago an acquaintance recounted to me the
details of a visit which he had paid at Kelmscott House
in Hammersmith with the view of seeing William Morris in
the flesh. It was on one of those Sunday afternoons when the
poet was at home to friends and visitors. Mr. Emery Walker
was present, as might be surmised by anyone who knows how
warm a friendship had sprung up between that high authority
on printing and the founder of the Kelmscott Press. My
friend tells me he introduced himself as an ardent admirer of
Morris's writings, and mentioned that he was acquainted with
a man named Buxton Forman who had for years been forming a Morris collection, and who in fact made a point of
buying whatever the poet might put forth. Morris, says my
informant, turned to Mr. Emery Walker with the characteristic
observation, " Useful kind of a man, that ! eh, Walker ?"

Now as I had known the poet at least a quarter of a century
at the time, and Mr. Walker perhaps half as long, the humour
of Morris in accepting me as a discovery, from a complete
stranger, seemed to me, and still seems, perfectly delightful.
It was all I ever aspired to be, " a useful kind of a man"; and,
if the assiduity with which I have followed up the quest, ever
since reading in *The Times* newspaper for the 11th of April
1868 a long review with many extracts from *The Life and
Death of Jason*, shall be found to have produced the means of
giving a complete account of Morris's publications, I shall be
able to believe that the revered and regretted poet spoke a true
word as well as a humorous one that Sunday afternoon at
Hammersmith. Craving pardon for this waste of the student's

or book-hunter's time on an egotistical preliminary anecdote,
I pass to my utility work of telling the story of the books—or
rather trying to make them tell their own story, so far as
dates, contents, and material features are concerned.

The tale begins when Morris was an Oxford undergraduate,
and had already written a great deal both of poetry and of
prose.   It was but natural that he should have taken up
warmly a scheme for starting a periodical of a somewhat
ambitious kind for a University magazine; and, when once it
was decided to found *The Oxford and Cambridge Magazine,* he
was liberal both with funds and with contributions—far more
with prose than with verse, however.   The first number of the
magazine appeared in January 1856
and the last in December of the same
year.   There are twelve in all, for it
was a monthly magazine : it was printed
in London at the Chiswick Press in a very sightly
manner, in double columns, and sent out in green
printed wrappers, each of which has the " Contents "
of the number on the first page.   These wrappers are
nicely arranged and executed : within an agreeable
old-fashioned " typographical border," of which this
is a specimen corner, are printed the name of the magazine, the " Contents," the publishers' imprint, etc.   The top
line (of No. I, for instance) is "No. I. JANUARY, 1856.
PRICE 1*s.*"   Then the title is given thus :

THE

Orford & Cambridge Magazine.

CONDUCTED BY MEMBERS OF THE
TWO UNIVERSITIES.

The " Contents " of the number follows ; then the publi-

cation lines, "LONDON :/ BELL AND DALDY, FLEET
STREET." All this is within the border : outside it is the
printer's imprint—at left " PRINTED BY C. WHITTINGHAM," at
right " TOOKS COURT, CHANCERY LANE." There are advertizements of a miscellaneous kind, both printed on the wrappers
and inserted between them and the outer sheets of the publication. Pages 2, 3 and 4 of the wrappers were invariably
covered with advertizements. The price was one shilling for
each number. In the last number a title-page and classified
table of contents were given. The title is as follows :

(1)

THE

OXFORD AND CAMBRIDGE
MAGAZINE
For 1856.

CONDUCTED BY MEMBERS OF THE TWO
UNIVERSITIES.

LONDON :
BELL AND DALDY, FLEET STREET.
1856.

As a rule, when copies of the work occur, the numbers have been
stripped of wrappers and other extraneous matter and bound
up with this title-page and "Contents" duly placed at the beginning. Such is the normal book : he who finds a set with
the wrappers preserved is fortunate among book-hunters ; he
who secures a clean set of unbound numbers, with wrappers
and advertizements and all just as issued, is still more to be

envied ; but he who can add to such a set the two fine photographs from Woolner's medallions of Tennyson and Carlyle, which the publishers of the magazine offered to subscribers, to bind with it if so minded, may be counted happy.

The book is a demy 8vo. The verso of the title is blank. The list of contents fills pages iii and iv, the text pages 1 to 776, which ends with the imprint (below a thin rule)—" CHISWICK PRESS : C. WHITTINGHAM, TOOKS COURT,/ CHANCERY LANE." Each number starts with a " dropped head " filled up by one of those charming ornaments,—the same each time,—designed some forty-five or fifty years ago by Charles Whittingham's daughter Charlotte (now Mrs. B. F. Stevens), assisted by her sister Elizabeth Eleanor Whittingham. The ornament selected from the series was that here reproduced : it

was originally engraved by Mary Byfield, and still holds its own among the many choice things of the Chiswick Press.

The ornamental heading was followed by the title of the

magazine and the title of the particular article, as usual ; and a pretty ornamental letter, thirteen sixteenths of an inch square, leads off the first article in each of the first two numbers. In the first number it happens to be a W. The other articles in each number begin with a similar letter, a little over eleven sixteenths of an inch square. The article on Tennyson chances

to start with an A. The distinctive larger-sized capital for the first article was abandoned with No. III. The pages are numbered at the outer corner in Arabic figures ; the head-lines are the titles of the various articles ; the abbreviated name of the month is at the right-hand end of each verso head-line ; and the left-hand end of each recto head-line has the year-date, 1856—month and year enclosed in square brackets.

The classified table of contents is as follows :—

CONTENTS.

In the early seventies, if not sooner, I obtained the set in
wrappers (as issued) used for the present description ; and at
that time I made a manuscript list of the principal authors,
specifying their contributions, as far as I was able to ascertain
them.　As Morris himself was my authority for that list, it is
well to print it here,—incomplete as it is ; for it is the measure
of the information he was then able to give from memory.
Morris did not profess to be certain about all the ascriptions in
this list ; and it turns out on investigation to be wrong in
several particulars.　Canon R. W. Dixon and Mr. Cormell
Price wrote some, but not all, of the pieces attributed to them ;
and Dean Jex Blake did not contribute at all.　Judge Lushing-

ton has a list made many years ago upon credible information.
It adds the names of several contributors to those given in
Morris's list,—as Sir Godfrey Lushington, Professor Lewis
Campbell, the late Bernard Cracroft, and Mr. Robert Campbell;
and another list adds the name of Dr. Aldis Wright. Here,
however, is the Morris list:—

PRINCIPAL CONTRIBUTORS

TO THE

OXFORD AND CAMBRIDGE MAGAZINE.

Neither of the foregoing tables of course gives any view of the arrangement of each number. In that matter much care was displayed. There was but one (No. XI) which did not contain a contribution or more from Morris; and it is worth while to state here the contents of each number. As a matter of editorial independence, be it recorded that the first thing printed on the inside of the front wrapper, in each of the first three numbers, is this :—

"Communications to be addressed to the Editor, care of Messrs. Bell and Daldy, 186, Fleet Street. It is requested that no gratuitous Copies of Books be sent for Review."

Bribery and corruption, even in the mild form of review copies, were to be sternly repressed! In the following lists of contents the names of the writers, known or supposed, are given in square brackets. Ascriptions about which any doubt has been suggested are marked with a note of interrogation.

CONTENTS OF No. I.

No. I consists simply of 64 pages and the printed wrapper.

CONTENTS OF No. II.

Besides 64 pages and the printed wrapper, No. II contains
a notice on a slip, about the article on the Barrier Kingdoms.

CONTENTS OF No. III.

No. III contains 64 pages, and, between the last page and
the wrapper, four extra pages of advertizements on the green
wrapper-paper.

CONTENTS OF No. IV.

There are 66 pages in No. IV. Inside the recto wrapper is
fastened a sixteen-page pamphlet which, though meant for an
advertizement, is not without interest. It is "A Sketch/ of the/
Political History of the Past/ Three Years,/ in connexion with/
The Press Newspaper,/ and/ the Part it has taken on the lead-
ing/ Questions of the Time./   London :/ Press Office—110,
Strand./   1856." The pamphlet ends with a reprint of an
article from the paper—an attack on John Bright written in

imitation of the trenchant style of Swift. An advertizement of
The Press printed inside the verso wrapper of the magazine
divulges the name of the publisher: it was Alfred JOR!
Between the pamphlet and the magazine is pasted a slip bearing this notice :—

Notice. *Now Ready, price* 1s. *each,*

A PHOTOGRAPHIC PORTRAIT OF THOMAS CARLYLE;
from a Medallion by T. WOOLNER; mounted so as to bind
with the *Oxford and Cambridge Magazine.*

LONDON :—BELL AND DALDY, 186, FLEET STREET.

CONTENTS OF No. V.

No. V consists of 64 pages and the wrapper, with an eight-
page advertizement of the Scottish Provident Institution
inserted at the end—printed in blue.

CONTENTS OF No. VI.

No. VI has 66 pages. At page 2 of the wrapper a mysterious
correspondent, " C," is requested to send his address to the
Editor. Between the last page of the number and the third
page of the wrapper are inserted an eight-page advertizement
of *The Westminster Review,* a four-page hand-bill about Taylor's
Specific Liniment and The American Sugar-coated Pills, and
another four-page hand-bill half of which is devoted to a

further exposition of the virtues of those pills, and the other half to Messrs. Cassell's publications—the whole, medicines and literature, specially commended for family use !

CONTENTS OF No. VII.

No. VII reverts to the simple tradition of 64 pages and a wrapper, but condescends to advertize pictorially "le miroir face et nuque"—the " New Patent Toilet Glass," an ordinary dressing-table glass, but with an arm projecting forward from the top, and a small round mirror so hung from the arm that a most unpreraphaelite lady, gazing in the main glass, sees, above the reflexion of her face, a lunette containing the image of the back of her head and neck. The poem here called *Hands* reappears as a part of *Rapunzel* in *The Defence of Guenevere and Other Poems.*

CONTENTS OF No. VIII.

No. VIII has but 64 pages again and no "miroir face et nuque" on the wrapper. In some copies the leaf on which pages 465 and 466 appear was incorrectly printed by what " Lewis Carroll " would call mixture of the bowsprit with the rudder,—that is to say the bottom line of the right column was put at the top of the left column, and the top line of the left column was put at the head of the right. A cancel-leaf was printed, and is sometimes found at the end of No. XII.

CONTENTS OF No. IX.

No. IX again has the normal 64 pages; but the four-page liniment and pills paper reappears at the end; and so does Our Lady of the Looking Glass on page 4 of the wrapper.

CONTENTS OF No. X.

No. X is also a normal number of 64 pages and wrapper; but no lady this time contemplates simultaneously the fatal beauty of her face and nape.

CONTENTS OF No. XI.

No. XI has an extra half-sheet, 72 pages in all. Opposite page 2 of the wrapper is pasted a slip bearing the following notice:—

Notice. *Now Ready, price 1s. each,*

PHOTOGRAPHIC PORTRAITS OF THOMAS CARLYLE, AND ALFRED TENNYSON; from Medallions by T. WOOLNER; mounted so as to bind with the *Oxford and Cambridge Magazine.*

LONDON:—BELL AND DALDY, 186, FLEET STREET.

On page 4 of the wrapper Our Lady of the Mirror makes her third and last appearance.

No. XII contains 70 pages of fresh matter, the title-page and contents (2 leaves) and the cancel for pages 465-6 already mentioned,—that is to say 76 pages in all.

In this final number some one played Morris an unwarrantable trick. The third paragraph of his story called *Golden Wings*, page 733, should open with the words:—" I have talked to old knights since who fought in that battle, and who told me that it was all about a lady that they fought ;" but the wag whom I am unable to specify substituted "an old lady " for " a lady "; and so the passage was printed.

I have not succeeded in fixing the exact date of Morris's next contribution to literature. Its title-page is plainly enough dated 1858; but whether it belongs to the early part of that year or the latter part of the year before, it does not seem possible to say. It is but a thin little pamphlet, and cannot be traced in the books of Messrs. George Bell and Sons, the imprint of whose predecessors, Messrs. Bell and Daldy, it bears. Neither is it traceable at the Chiswick Press, at which *The Oxford and Cambridge Magazine* and Morris's first two volumes of poetry were printed. It does not, however, look like Chiswick Press printing ; and so small a thing may have been got done anywhere. The title-page is

(2)

SIR GALAHAD

A CHRISTMAS MYSTERY.

BY

WILLIAM MORRIS.

LONDON :

BELL AND DALDY, 186, FLEET STREET.

1858.

This very rare little tract is a foolscap 8vo. consisting of half-title, " SIR GALAHAD," title, and 14 pages of text. Pages 6 to 18 are numbered in the outer top corners as usual ; and the head-lines read throughout " SIR GALAHAD, A CHRISTMAS MYSTERY," in capitals and small capitals. It appears to have been thought worth while to make a *fac-simile* reprint :

(3) it is not an absolute *fac-simile*, of course ; for there is probably no such thing in the wide world. This one, though very cleverly executed, is not difficult to detect when set beside the original. The paper is thinner and whiter in the reprint than in the real thing,—looks more recent, altogether, and does not show up the type so well. Then there are typographical differences. In the half-title of the reprint is an L with a broken serif : it is perfect in the original. In the title of the reprint the date is three sixteenths of an inch below the publication line, whereas in the original the distance is one thirty-second of an inch less. In the " dropped head " at page 5 the M in CHRISTMAS is broken in the reprint though perfect in the original. But perhaps the easiest test for a wary collector is to be found in the third line of page 16, where the word *hauberk* is spelt without a final *e* in the reprint, although Morris spelt it with a final *e*, *hauberke*, both in the original tract and in *The Defence of Guenevere and other Poems* (1858). One more difference is that the original is a sheet and a single leaf, while the reprint has, in such copies as I have met with, a blank leaf attached to the last leaf of the text. Of course I cannot say that all copies are so, or that no copy of the original will ever turn up with such a blank leaf at the end ; but there is that difference between copies of the two issues as known to me. This poem was naturally included in the volume issued in the course of 1858 under the title of *The Defence of Guenevere, and other Poems*, which also contained poems already issued in the magazine. When the contents of that most remarkable book were being composed, Mr. Swinburne, also at Oxford, had in hand, perhaps in print, his *Rosamond*, which, however, was at all events not " submitted to the censure of the ingenuous " public till 1860, when it appeared with *The Queen-Mother*. Whether notes were compared by means of manuscripts or of private prints, certain it is that each of the two young poets was greatly impressed with the other's work, each giving the palm to his friendly rival. Further, each dedicated

his book to Dante Gabriel Rossetti. The title-page of Morris's first substantive volume reads thus :—

(4)

THE

DEFENCE OF GUENEVERE,

AND OTHER POEMS.

By WILLIAM MORRIS.

LONDON :

BELL AND DALDY, 186, FLEET STREET.

1858.

This is a foolscap 8vo. of 248 pages beside four preliminary leaves, namely a half-title reading THE DEFENCE OF GUENEVERE,/ AND OTHER POEMS, title with blank verso, dedication with blank verso, and two pages of "Contents." The dedication is—

TO MY FRIEND,

DANTE GABRIEL ROSSETTI,

PAINTER,

I DEDICATE THESE POEMS.

The list of contents is as follows :—

CONTENTS.

There is a five-line list of Errata[1] printed on a slip and, in original copies "as issued," attached by one end to page 1. The book is printed in the ornate style general at that time in Chiswick Press Books. The pages are numbered in Arabic figures in the outer top corners; and the title of each poem is printed as a head-line, recto and verso, in italics. At the foot of page 248, below a thin rule, is the imprint "CHISWICK PRESS:— PRINTED BY C. WHITTINGHAM,/ TOOKS COURT, CHANCERY LANE." The cover is of dark brown diced cloth with brownish drab end-papers, and is lettered in gilt at the back "THE/ DEFENCE/ OF/ GUENEVERE/ MORRIS/ LONDON/

---

[1] ERRATA

Page 13, bottom line, for *the*, read *to*.
„ 75, line 10, for *yard*, read *gard*.
„ 88, four lines from bottom, for *harms*, read *harm*.
„ 106, line 1, for *yo*, read *yo*.
„ 220, line 10, for *yay me, Robert*, read *yay me Robert*.

BELL & DALDY." Though 500 copies were printed, it is now not easy to buy a copy.

During the days of the great fame which greeted Morris on the succession of *The Earthly Paradise* to *Jason*, he had what I cannot doubt to have been a genuine misprision of this delightful little book. With his usual unerring instinct, however, he refused to revise it; and it was with difficulty that he was persuaded, by the year 1875, to allow it to be reprinted in one of those agreeable crown 8vo. volumes which issued from 33 King Street and 29 New Bond Street. The title-page of the reprint reads thus :—

(5)

THE/ DEFENCE OF GUENEVERE,/ AND OTHER POEMS./ BY WILLIAM MORRIS./ *(Reprinted without alteration from the edition of 1858.)/* LONDON :/ ELLIS & WHITE, 29, NEW BOND STREET./ 1875.

This crown 8vo. book is a page-for-page reprint of the foolscap 8vo., but in the plain style of typography adopted by Strangeways and Walden for *The Earthly Paradise* and other poems by Morris. At the foot of page 248 it has the imprint, not of Strangeways and Walden, but of Mr. Roberts, thus — " PRINTED BY ROBERT ROBERTS, BOSTON, LINCOLNSHIRE." It seems to have been set up from a copy of the first edition wanting the *Errata* slip ; and so literally was the poet's determination, not to revise his early work, carried out, that with one exception his corrections of 1858 were not made, and the text suffers accordingly. The one correction made, out of the five directed, was *go* for *yo ;* and that a printer of Mr. Roberts's stamp could scarcely help making. The book was issued in an unusually fine " Morris-green " cloth, unblocked, with a printed back-label, reading " THE/ DEFENCE/ OF/ GUEN-EVERE/ *And other Poems/* BY/ W. MORRIS./ 8s." There were twenty-five copies on Whatman's paper, of demy 8vo. size, done up in grey paper boards with cream-white paper backs and printed labels.

The poet's heart must, one would think, have softened at last towards this child of his early manhood, or how should he have sent it forth again in all the beauty of Kelmscott Press

printing ? This he certainly did, setting it in the Golden type,
and doing all that might be done to make its array as choice
as the poetry itself. Like many other Kelmscott books, this,
which is a small 8vo., has no title-page properly so called;
and we have to fall back on the half-title and colophon. The
half-title is

(6)

THE DEFENCE OF GUENEVERE,/ AND OTHER
POEMS. BY WILLIAM/ MORRIS.

On the verso of this is the list of contents; and the leaf
appears to be the fourth in a half sheet; for it is preceded by three blank leaves beside the end-paper. The first
page of the text has one of those beautiful ornamental
borders now so renowned, and is printed in black capitals
with a large ornamental initial, and preceded by the rubric
"HERE BEGINNETH THE DEFENCE OF GUEN-
EVERE." The poems occupy 169 pages, are set without
head-lines, but with rubricated titles at the top of the outer
margins. There are Arabic page-numbers at the foot, ornamental capitals galore designed by the author, occasional other
ornaments; and all names of speakers, stage directions, and
refrains, are printed in red. The colophon is

> HERE ends The Defence of Guenevere, and/ other Poems,
> written by William Morris; and/ printed by him at the
> Kelmscott Press, 14, Upper Mall, Hammersmith, in the
> County of/ Middlesex; & finished on the 2nd day of April,/
> of the Year 1892./ Sold by Reeves & Turner, 196,
> Strand, London.

This is followed by the smaller book-mark; and the page,
being the verso of the 5th leaf in signature m, is followed by
three blank leaves completing the sheet, beside the end-paper.
The book is a very desirable one: it is of those in which the
thin, crisp, hand-made paper is left wholly untrimmed. It is
bound in limp vellum with silk ties of colours varying in
different copies; and, instead of being gilt-lettered, the word
"Guenevere" is written in ink up the back in bold medieval

letters. This was done by Mr. F. S. Ellis for the whole issue. There were 300 copies on paper and 10 on vellum.

The Kelmscott *Guenevere* would have been still more treasurable if the opportunity had been taken to purify the text. If Morris read the proofs he must have done so without much realization of his early work, and but just enough to attend to the due artistic disposition of the type. The "copy" given to the Kelmscott printers was one of the 1875 reissue, marked in regard to the ornaments to be used. The first *erratum* on the list of 1858 deals with the passage always printed

> my eyes,
> Wept all away the grey, may bring some sword
> To drown you in your blood ;

and, when the poet's intention was fresh in his mind, he directed that we were to read "wept all away *to* grey." That is no doubt the true meaning ; but the passage was not so printed either by Mr. Roberts in 1875 or by Morris himself in 1892, and is still corrupt. The same is true of the line in *Sir Peter Harpdon's End,*

> A sprawling lonely yard with rotten walls,

which retains the word *yard* though Morris directed the substitution of *gard* in 1858. The next correction from the 1858 *Errata* slip, though not made at Boston, was made at the Kelmscott Press : it is in the passage

> 't will harm your cause
> To hang knights of good name, harm here in France

in which the second *harm* was formerly misprinted *harms.* The fourth correction of 1858, *go* for *yo*, was of course duly made at Hammersmith as formerly at Boston ; but the most important of all is the fifth, which was made at neither press. In *The Haystack in the Floods*, where Godmar is taunting Jehane, and breaks off to direct his people to gag her Knight Robert, who of course could not otherwise keep silence, the words of all three editions are

> Eh—gag me, Robert !—sweet my friend,
> This were indeed a piteous end.

The direction of 1858 to substitute "gag me Robert" should

be carried out at the first opportunity. Godmar of course does not, even in irony, invite Robert to gag him, but for convenience tells his people to gag Robert for him, *me* being the dative, as in " saddle me the ass." At page 57 of the Kelmscott edition the line

> Do you care altogether more for France

is properly substituted for

> Do you care altogether more than France

in which *than* was an undetected error of the editions of 1858 and 1875. On the other hand, at page 60 is a new error: the line

> And yet you will be hung like a cur dog

is disfigured by the omission of *yet*.

As Master-printer Morris jotted down on the sheets of Master-printer Robert Roberts of Boston in Lincolnshire instructions to the Kelmscott workmen concerning the ornamental letters and " sides " they were to set against the text of these early poems, the eye of Master-poet Morris opened once, at least, and fell upon a cockney rhyme. It was almost at the end of the book that this critical awakening took place. He saw that in the tender little poem called *Summer Dawn* the final set of rhymes stood thus :—

> Through the long twilight they pray for the dawn,
> Round the lone house in the midst of the corn.

Of this couplet he struck out the first line, substituting

> They pray the long gloom through for daylight new-born

and did not, it seems, trouble himself further about the matter when the proofs came ; for the line was printed with a full-stop at the end and so disconnected from the line which follows it and completes the sense ! This poem had appeared without a title in *The Oxford and Cambridge Magazine*, where "the roses are dun " had been misprinted "the roses are dim." This was corrected in the *Guenevere* volume of 1858, wherein the title *Summer Dawn* was added ; but the rhyme " dawn " and " corn " survived till 1892. The correction then made recalled to my mind a friendly passage of arms I had with Morris in 1875 over the Virgil. He had used " wrath " and " forth " as a rhyme ; and I had asked him to alter it— characterizing the rhyme in the usual manner. He wrote promising to consider the point, but adding that, " not having had the misfortune to be born in Aberdeen," he had " no need to call happier people cocknies." He went on to say he would defend the rhyme in another man's work if not used too often because " *no* South Englishman makes any difference in ordinary talk between dawn and morn for instance." I fear it was only the criterion of frequency that was applied in 1892 to *Summer Dawn* ; for he had this very rhyme twice in that little poem, and struck it out in one place, letting it stand in the other.

Since the transfer of Morris's works from Messrs. Reeves and Turner to Messrs. Longmans, Green, and Co., the *Guenevere* volume, like other separate poetical books of (7) the author, has been issued with a printed label which, alone, connects the volumes as a set of ten. The label in this case reads " THE/ POETICAL/ WORKS OF/ WILLIAM/ MORRIS/ THE/ DEFENCE/ OF/ GUENEVERE/ AND OTHER POEMS/ *Six Shillings.*"

The Defence of Guenevere of 1858 must have sold very slowly ; for it was still to be had at Messrs. Bell and Daldy's after they had moved to York Street, Covent Garden, and published the *Jason*. But it was difficult to get soon after the first volume of *The Earthly Paradise* appeared, and is now rather eagerly sought,—most collectors still preferring the *editio princeps* even to the Kelmscott impression.

QUEEN SQUARE

THE LIFE AND DEATH OF JASON
THE EARTHLY PARADISE
SAGAS FROM THE ICELANDIC

THE WOOD-CUT OR BOOK-MARK MADE FOR "THE EARTHLY PARADISE."

QUEEN SQUARE:

The Life and Death of Jason—The Earthly Paradise—
Sagas from the Icelandic.

Morris's next book, the superlative merits of which were
destined to be quickly recognized both by the critics and by the
reading public, was to have been called *The Deeds of Jason*;
but, by the time he had it ready for publication, that title was
rejected in favour of a longer one. By January 1867 the epic
in seventeen books was finished, and an edition of 500 copies
put through the press with the following title:

(8)

THE LIFE AND DEATH
OF JASON

A POEM

By WILLIAM MORRIS.

LONDON:
BELL AND DALDY,
YORK STREET, COVENT GARDEN.
1867.

It is an agreeable crown 8vo. printed on a thinnish creamy
laid paper. The seventeen books occupy 363 pages, preceded
simply by a half-title, THE LIFE AND DEATH/ OF
JASON, the title-page itself, and a slip bearing a ten-line list
of *errata*, which was bound up with the sheets so as to get a
secure place between the title and the opening of the book.
In this first edition, an "Argument," thirteen lines of small

type, precedes the opening of the poem on page 1. It is an argument of the whole story ; and the individual books are not furnished with arguments. In later editions, they are. The pages are numbered in Arabic figures in the outer top corners ; and the head-lines, which are in italic capitals, read " *THE LIFE AND DEATH* " on versos, " *OF JASON* " on rectos. At the foot of page 363, below a thin rule, is the imprint— CHISWICK PRESS :—PRINTED BY WHITTINGHAM AND WILKINS,/ TOOKS COURT, CHANCERY LANE. On an unpaged leaf at the end is an announcement that *The Earthly Paradise* is in preparation. The book is bound in unblocked cherry-coloured cloth, smooth, but not excessively shiny, with a printed label reading " The/ Life/ and/ Death/ of/ Jason/ A Poem/ by/ William Morris/ Bell and Daldy." The announcement of *The Earthly Paradise,* an important document, is as follows :

In preparation, by the same Author.

THE EARTHLY PARADISE.

CONTAINING THE FOLLOWING TALES
IN VERSE.

PROLOGUE,—THE WANDERERS; OR, THE SEARCH FOR ETERNAL YOUTH.
THE STORY OF THESEUS.
THE SON OF CROESUS.
THE STORY OF CUPID AND PSYCHE.
THE KING'S TREASURE-HOUSE.
THE STORY OF ORPHEUS AND EURYDICE.
THE STORY OF PYGMALION.
ATALANTA'S RACE.
THE DOOM OF KING ACRISIUS.
THE STORY OF RHODOPE.
THE DOLPHINS AND THE LOVERS.
THE FORTUNES OF GYGES.
THE STORY OF BELLEROPHON.
THE WATCHING OF THE FALCON.
THE LADY OF THE LAND.
THE HILL OF VENUS.
THE SEVEN SLEEPERS.
THE MAN WHO NEVER LAUGHED AGAIN.
THE PALACE EAST OF THE SUN.
THE QUEEN OF THE NORTH.
THE STORY OF DOROTHEA.
THE WRITING ON THE IMAGE.
THE PROUD KING.
THE RING GIVEN TO VENUS.
THE MAN BORN TO BE KING.
EPILOGUE.

Although that is not the precise program which was followed, it was the inventory of further intellectual property which fell into the hands of Morris's old friend Mr. F. S. Ellis together with the beautiful poem to which it was appended. Up to that time, Morris had risked his own money on his poetic ventures. On seeing the *Jason*, Mr. Ellis, then a bookseller and publisher in King Street, Covent Garden, told the poet that, had he seen the poem in manuscript, he would have published it at his own risk, and that he was ready to follow that course in respect of the larger work in preparation. In the mean while the *Jason* was doing well enough to induce Messrs. Bell and Daldy, who had published both it and the *Guenevere* volume on commis-(9–10) sion, to arrange with the author for the payment of a fixed sum for the right to print on their own account 1000 copies. *Jason* was therefore set up again for their account ; a second edition of 500 was printed, and published in December 1867 ; stereotype plates were made ; and, in October 1868, a third edition was issued, printed from those plates. This, however, was the last book published for Morris by Messrs. Bell and Daldy ; for the long-standing arrangement with Mr. Ellis began that very year.

The book being stereotyped, the plates were transferred from the Chiswick Press to Messrs. Strangeways and Walden when the fourth edition was called for in 1869 ; and Mr. Ellis, who had bought the plates, and had in the meantime issued the first volume of *The Earthly Paradise*, published, still in crown 8vo., the edition of which the title-page reads thus :—

(11)

THE/ LIFE AND DEATH OF JASON/ A POEM./ [Wood-cut] By/ WILLIAM MORRIS,/ Author of The Earthly Paradise./ *fourth edition./* London : F. S. Ellis, *33 King Street, Covent Garden./* mdccclxix./ [*All Rights reserved.*]

Of this edition 1000 ordinary copies were printed. They had passed through the press by July 1869, and were issued in red cloth, labelled, as usual.

Twenty-five demy 8vo. copies were printed on Whatman's hand-made paper ; and these, from which the date was omitted, were put up in grey paper boards with white backs, and printed labels. A single demy 8vo. copy on machine-made paper (wove) was printed with the date, and put up in light brown cloth with the ordinary printed label. As this is something of a curiosity, I give the title-page below :—

THE

LIFE AND DEATH OF JASON

A POEM.

BY

WILLIAM MORRIS,

AUTHOR OF THE EARTHLY PARADISE.

FOURTH EDITION.

London : F. S. ELLIS, *33 King Street, Covent Garden.*

MDCCCLXIX.

[*All Rights reserved.*]

In January 1872 another 1000 ordinary copies issued from the press. These (perhaps with some left over (12–13–14) from the 1000 done in 1869) are believed to have formed the fifth, sixth, and seventh editions. The sixth has a half-title and title like the previous ones, but with the words *SIXTH EDITION* above the imprint, which is "LONDON :/ ELLIS AND GREEN,/ 33 KING STREET, COVENT GARDEN, W.C./ 1872." The imprint at the foot of page 376 is "LONDON :/ Printed by JOHN STRANGEWAYS, Castle St. Leicester Sq." On the verso of the leaf is the usual book-mark as on the title. The book was issued in the usual red cloth, but with a blind single-rule border on the sides and gilt-lettered at the back "THE/ LIFE/ AND/

DEATH/ OF/ JASON/ W. MORRIS." The end-papers are white. The eighth edition was revised : its title-page is

(15)

THE/ LIFE AND DEATH OF JASON/ A POEM./ [Wood-cut.] BY/ WILLIAM MORRIS,/ Author of The Earthly Paradise./ *Eighth Edition, revised by the Author./* LONDON :/ ELLIS AND WHITE, 29 NEW BOND STREET, W./ 1882./ [*All Rights reserved.*]

Two thousand ordinary and 25 large-paper copies were printed. This issue again consists of 376 pages of poetry preceded by a half-title, "THE/ LIFE AND DEATH OF JASON" and a title with the complete "argument" on the verso, and followed by four pages of advertizements. The imprint at the foot of page 376, below a thin rule, is "LONDON :/ Printed by Strangeways & Sons, Tower Street, Upper St. Martin's Lane." The book is bound in unblocked red cloth, with white end-papers, and has a printed label reading "THE/ LIFE/ AND/ DEATH/ OF/ JASON./ W. MORRIS./ Eighth Edition./ 8s." The large-paper copies were done up in the usual grey boards

backed with white and labelled. A fire which broke out at the Strangeways printing-house had destroyed, *inter alia*, the bold block cut by Morris for the book-mark of this period ; and the design had been badly repro-duced, as shown by the fac-simile here-with.

In 1895 Morris is-sued *Jason* in a new form — one of the sumptuous quartos of the Kelmscott press (folio shape), printed in black and

4

red in the Troy type and adorned by two wood-cuts after Sir Edward Burne-Jones's designs. The title reads thus :—

(16)

THE LIFE AND DEATH OF JASON./ A POEM. BY WILLIAM MORRIS.

The colophon is as follows: "Here endeth the Life and Death of Jason, Written by William Morris, and printed by the said William Morris at the Kelmscott Press, Upper Mall, Hammersmith, in the County of Middlesex, and finished on the 25th day of May, 1895. Sold by William Morris at the Kelmscott Press." Besides the 353 pages of the book proper, there are leaves at the beginning and at the end forming part of the sheets of the book. The wood-cuts face pages 5 and 354; and the larger Kelmscott book-mark is to be found at page 357. The binding, by Leighton, is of limp vellum with silk ties, lettered in gold at the back "THE/ LIFE AND DEATH/ OF JASON/ BY WILLIAM/ MORRIS"; and the end-papers are complete sheets of the same paper as the book (four leaves at each end, including the paste-down).

It was not to be supposed that a poet of Morris's extraordinary productiveness and versatility confined himself within even such limits as were indicated in the announcement of *The Earthly Paradise* made at the end of *Jason.* Some of the overflow of his energy, while prosecuting the extensive scheme of poetic romance by which he was long best known, enriched the pages of periodicals. As early as August 1869 a longish minor poem, *The God of the Poor*, appeared in *The Fortnightly Review*,—to reappear as a pamphlet in the Socialist period of his activity. In October 1868 the same periodical contained that charming dialogue of youths and maidens *The Two Sides of the River.*

The first instalment of the great cycle of tales which we know as *The Earthly Paradise* came out in 1868 without any very obtrusive indications of incompleteness, although people who took the trouble to read the advertizements at the end of this volume of nearer 700 than 600 pages had no valid excuse for thinking that their newly acquired treasure was a complete book in itself. It was for this book that the graceful and admirably composed design of the three lady minstrels in a garden was made and cut upon wood by the poet himself; although the use of it was at once extended to *Jason*. The title-page of the first volume of *The Earthly Paradise* is as follows:

(17)

THE

EARTHLY PARADISE

A POEM.

BY

WILLIAM MORRIS,

AUTHOR OF THE LIFE AND DEATH OF JASON.

London: F. S. ELLIS, 33 *King Street, Covent Garden.*

MDCCCLXVIII

[*All Rights reserved.*]

It is a crown 8vo. volume containing 676 pages of poetry. There are four preliminary leaves, namely a half-title THE EARTHLY PARADISE, the title with an imprint on the verso, LONDON :/ STRANGEWAYS AND WALDEN, PRINTERS,/ 28 CASTLE ST. LEICESTER SQ., a leaf bearing on the recto the words "TO/ MY WIFE/ I DEDICATE THIS BOOK," and "A Table of Contents" occupying two pages. Facing page 676, the book-mark is repeated on a leaf which has the imprint of Strangeways and Walden again on the verso. This is followed by four pages of advertizements, one about the rest of *The Earthly Paradise*, one about *Jason*, and two about other works published by Mr. Ellis. The book was issued in dark green unblocked cloth with white end-papers and a printed label reading "THE EARTHLY/ PARADISE/ A POEM./ BY/ WILLIAM MORRIS./ *Price* 14s."

There were 25 copies printed on Whatman's hand-made
paper of demy 8vo. size. This made the book too thick to be
done up in one volume; and it was divided into two. The
title-page was not altered; but the Strangeways imprint was
inserted on the verso of page 343 to mark the close of Vol. I;
and on the recto of page 344 a half-title was printed, reading
THE EARTHLY PARADISE/ A POEM./ BY WILLIAM
MORRIS./ VOL. II. The volumes were put up in blue paper
boards with cream-white backs, labelled THE EARTHLY/
PARADISE./ W. MORRIS./ I [II]. These and many, if
not all, of the large-paper books issued by Mr. Ellis from
Covent Garden and New Bond Street were done up by an
old-fashioned binder named Shaw in Featherstone Buildings.
They were so done as to present a very agreeable appearance.
The bands showed through the backs; and one felt some con-
fidence that the unpretentious sewing was destined to hold the
sheets together as long as one wished. I have never yet seen
any copies coming to pieces as ordinary trade sewing allows
books to do.

In order to note changes of program as we go along it is well
to set forth what we have in this first instalment and what it
was intended to add thereto. Here, therefore, from pages vii
and viii, is

A TABLE OF CONTENTS

Up to this time (April 1868) the intention of completing the book in two volumes appears to have held; for the notice at the end of the first volume is as follows:

IN PREPARATION

THE

SECOND AND CONCLUDING VOLUME

OF

THE EARTHLY PARADISE

WHICH WILL CONTAIN

THE FOLLOWING TALES IN VERSE.

THE STORY OF THESEUS.
THE HILL OF VENUS.
THE STORY OF ORPHEUS AND EURYDICE.
THE STORY OF DOROTHEA.
THE FORTUNES OF GYGES.
THE PALACE EAST OF THE SUN.
THE DOLPHINS AND THE LOVERS.
THE MAN WHO NEVER LAUGHED AGAIN.
THE STORY OF RHODOPE.
AMYS AND AMILLION.
THE STORY OF BELLEROPHON.
THE RING GIVEN TO VENUS.
THE EPILOGUE TO THE EARTHLY PARADISE.

The edition of 1000 copies was quickly exhausted; and a further issue of 750 copies was ready by about midsummer. To this issue the description of the first applies, save (18) that the words " SECOND EDITION " are inserted over the publisher's name in the title-page and under the author's name on the label, while the advertizements about *The Earthly Paradise* and *Jason* alone appear on a single leaf at the end, and the miscellaneous advertizements on a smaller leaf pasted on the first end-paper. In August 1868, 1250 more (19–20) copies were printed; and these are believed to have formed the third and fourth editions, to each of which the same general description applies as to the first and second. The fifth edition was in two volumes printed on thicker paper, laid instead of wove. Of this edition 1000 copies were printed. They were through the press by November (21) 1869. The variations of title page from previous issues are above and beneath the publication line,—" Part I. [II.]/ *FIFTH EDITION*,"—and " MDCCCLXX." The first Part has

half-title, title, Dedication, and "Contents," and pages 1 to 343
of the text, with the book-mark repeated on the verso of
page 343. The second part has a blank leaf, half-title, title,
"Contents," and 334 pages. Page 1 is a second half-title
"THE/ EARTHLY PARADISE./ MAY, JUNE, JULY,
AUGUST." The text begins on page 2. The usual imprint
(which is on the verso of each title) recurs at the foot of
page 334; and the book ends with the book-mark on the recto
of an otherwise blank leaf. The cloth cover is as usual; and
the hand-list of Morris's works is inserted at the beginning of
each volume. The back-labels read "THE/ EARTHLY/
PARADISE./ W. MORRIS./ Fifth Edition./ I. [II.]/
Price 8s."

During the year 1869 a further instalment of *The Earthly
Paradise* was issued, but not till November, and then dated
1870. In the mean time the poet had taken up with characteristic vigour the study of Icelandic literature. It was not
sufficient that he should read it: he must also transplant it
into our literature for the benefit of others. I shall never
forget the revelation of a new world of literary art which I
owed to him at that time. There were very few who did not
think his time wasted on those translations done in conjunction
with Mr. Magnússon. To me his time seemed so well employed that I obtained and read every one of the Sagas which
I could ascertain to have been translated into English, no
matter by whom; and I remember his telling me, together
with some information about this literature, that I was his
"first convert to Sagaism." Well, this "Sagaism" was a
very good thing for his own work: apart from the beauty of his
translations, the new fibre he assimilated from that hardy
literature was just what was wanted.

In *The Fortnightly Review* for January 1869, he and Mr.
Magnússon published their version of *The Saga of Gunnlaug
the Worm-tongue and Rafn the Skald, as the Priest Ari
Thorgilson the Learned has told it, who of all Men in Iceland
has been the deepest in Knowledge of Tales of Land-settling and
Olden Lore.* Mr. Morley was also fortunate enough to secure
for the April 1869 number of the Review a second dialogue
poem, *On The Edge of the Wilderness,* in all respects the
pendant of *The Two Sides of the River;* and in the same
month a poem in a similar style, *Hapless Love,* appeared in

Good Words. This was followed at a very short interval by a rendering of the *Saga of Grettir the Strong*, which was through the press by May 1869 as an independent book with the title—

(22)

GRETTIS SAGA

THE STORY

OF

GRETTIR THE STRONG

TRANSLATED FROM THE ICELANDIC

BY

EIRÍKR MAGNUSSON,

TRANSLATOR OF 'LEGENDS OF ICELAND;'

AND

WILLIAM MORRIS,

AUTHOR OF 'THE EARTHLY PARADISE.'

LONDON :

F. S. ELLIS, KING STREET, COVENT GARDEN.

MDCCCLXIX.

In this crown 8vo. volume, of which only 500 copies were printed, the introductory matter occupies pages i to xxiv and the Saga with Notes, Indexes, etc., 306 pages. The preliminary sheet and a half consist of a half-title *GRETTIS SAGA*, with a sonnet on the verso, title, preface (pages v to xvi), Chronology of the Story (pages xvii and xviii), Contents (pages xix to xxiv) ; and between this and the Saga is a two-page map engraved on wood by Morris in a bold style, entitled " *A MAP OF THE WEST/ PARTS OF ICELAND,/ WITH THE CHIEF/ STEADS NAMED IN/ THE STORY.*" The pages of the book are numbered in the outer corners with Arabic figures ; and the head-lines are, versos *THE STORY OF*, rectos *GRETTIR THE STRONG*, in italic capitals. At the foot of page 306, below a thin rule, is the imprint, "London: STRANGEWAYS AND WALDEN, Castle St. Leicester Sq." The binding was of pale drab cloth, unblocked, with white end-papers and a printed label at the back, reading "*GRETTIS SAGA*/ THE STORY OF/ GRETTIR/ THE STRONG/ E. MAGNÚSSON/ AND/ W. MORRIS/ 8s." A handbill advertizing the fourth edition of *The Earthly Paradise* on the recto and *Jason* on the verso, both with opinions of the press, is pasted inside the first cover. Twenty-five copies of *Grettir* were printed on Whatman's hand-made paper, in demy 8vo., and put up in blue paper boards with white paper backs and a printed label reading "THE STORY/ OF GRETTIR/ THE STRONG." Except for the doing-up and the size and quality of the paper, they differ in no way from the ordinary copies,—not having so much as a certificate. The story of the man so beautifully commemorated in the Sonnet[1] facing the title-page of *Grettis Saga* was followed before the end of November 1869 by the second instalment of the great tale-cycle still so popular. The title-page is:—

(23)

THE

EARTHLY PARADISE

A POEM.

BY

WILLIAM MORRIS,

AUTHOR OF THE LIFE AND DEATH OF JASON.

PART III.

London: F. S. ELLIS, 33 *King Street, Covent Garden.*

MDCCCLXX

[*All Rights reserved.*]

---

[1] The Sonnet form was an unusual one for Morris; and this example of it

Between the issue of *Grettir the Strong* and Part III of *The Earthly Paradise* the fourth edition of the first instalment had been exhausted. That instalment was now reprinted in two volumes (see page 55) on thickish laid paper, and called Part I and Part II, the new volume being called Part III. This Part III, printed on the same thickish paper as the fifth edition of Parts I and II, is of course a crown 8vo. volume, like the rest; and it consists of 528 pages with three preliminary leaves,—half-title, title, and " Contents "; the half-title and " Contents " are blank at the back ; but the title has at foot of the verso the imprint " LONDON :/ STRANGEWAYS AND WALDEN, PRINTERS,/ Castle St. Leicester Sq." The list of contents is as follows :

CONTENTS

Page 1 is a fresh half-title, " THE/ EARTHLY PARADISE./ SEPTEMBER, OCTOBER,/ NOVEMBER." On the verso of this, page 2, the new poetry begins. In style and detail of printing the volume is uniform with the previous one. Page 527 is simply the book-mark again ; and on page 528

has been unduly neglected for years past : —

> A life scarce worth the living, a poor fame
> Scarce worth the winning, in a wretched land,
> Where fear and pain go upon either hand,
> As toward the end men fare without an aim
> Unto the dull grey dark from whence they came :
> Let them alone, the unshadowed sheer rocks stand
> Over the twilight graves of that poor band,
> Who count so little in the great world's game !
> Nay with the dead I deal not ; this man lives,
> And that which carried him through good and ill,
> Stern against fate while his voice echoed still
> From rock to rock, now he lies silent, strives
> With wasting time, and through its long lapse gives
> Another friend to me, life's void to fill.

the printers imprint is repeated. These pages are not numbered. The volume was issued in unblocked green cloth boards, the cloth as near a match as could be got to that used for the first volume, with white end-papers and a printed label reading "THE/ EARTHLY/ PARADISE./ W. MORRIS./ III./ *Price* 12s." Inside the first cover was pasted a hand-bill advertizing the fifth edition of Parts I and II, this new Part III, *Grettir the Strong*, and the fourth edition of *Jason*, and announcing as in preparation the fourth and concluding Part of *The Earthly Paradise*, and "a New Edition of *The Defence of Guenevere*, and other Early Poems, with the addition of some pieces not hitherto collected." As we have already seen this promise was not fulfilled : *The Defence of Guenevere and other Poems* was simply reissued without alteration or addition. Of the ordinary copies of this second instalment (Part III) 2000 were printed ; but (24) some of these, I believe, formed the second edition. Of Part III 25 large paper copies uniform with those of Parts I and II were printed and divided into two volumes. The Strangeways imprint was inserted at the foot of page 273, which is followed by a blank page and a blank leaf ; and on the recto of page 274 is a half-title for "Vol. IV" like that for "Vol. II," the labels also being marked " III " and " IV."

A third edition of Part III (the whole second instalment) was wanted by August 1870, when 500 more issued from the press. Of these second and third editions there is (25) nothing to note, but the insertion of the words *second edition* and *third edition* in the title-pages and on the back-labels.

It does not come within the scope of this book to note all the American reprints of *The Earthly Paradise* and other works by Morris ; but at this point there is something unusual of transatlantic reproduction to be recorded. Messrs. Roberts Brothers of Boston, Mass., who published and still publish Morris's works in the United States, printed a handy edition of *The Earthly Paradise* from advance sheets supplied by the English publisher ; and, while issuing Part III of the (26) work, they took the opportunity of printing from the same types a separate pocket volume consisting of *The Lovers of Gudrun* alone. The importance of this poem as the first high attempt to convert one of the larger domestic Sagas of Iceland into a heroic poem is not easy to overrate. Landor had made an elegant enough thing out of the little Saga of Gunnlaug; but he did not capture the true Northern spirit as Morris did; and the Saga of the Laxdale Men, one of the most notable for varied domestic and historic interest, vivid characterization, and tragic action, gave Morris an opportunity of transplanting something really fresh into our poetic literature. This is one of the most significant points in the poet's literary career. As soon as he became truly possessed of this great *Laxdæla Saga*, all chance of getting *The Earthly Paradise* completed in two volumes was at an end; and a new scheme was inevitable. His magnificent version of that noble old story occupies wellnigh two hundred pages of the second instalment of his tale-cycle; and, in default of any independent English edition of *The Lovers of Gudrun*, the little book brought out at Boston, Mass., ranks as the first separate edition of the poem : its title-page is as follows :

(27)

THE

LOVERS OF GUDRUN.

A POEM.

By WILLIAM MORRIS.

REPRINTED FROM "THE EARTHLY PARADISE."

BOSTON:

ROBERTS BROTHERS.

1870.

The volume is in post 8vo., printed on a creamy laid paper. The poem occupies 138 pages, preceded by the title-page given above, on the verso of which is the following

PUBLISHERS' NOTE.

" ' The Lovers of Gudrun ' is one of the six stories comprising the Third Part of ' The Earthly Paradise,' and is reprinted from that volume for the convenience of tourists and others. The publishers have not thought it necessary to make any change in the paging."

At the foot of the page is the imprint " University Press : Welch, Bigelow, & Co.,/ Cambridge." Facing the title-page is a frontispiece representing Gudrun, " just come to her full height," standing betwixt the pillars of the Hall at Bathstead. At the end of the volume is a collection of "Tributes to William Morris, on the Publication of The Earthly Paradise." This is printed from the stereotyped plates of a 36-page pamphlet compiled by Messrs. Roberts Brothers from the English and American periodical press soon after the issue of the first volume of *The Earthly Paradise*. The title-page of the Tributes, and the advertizements at the back of it, are slightly altered from the original separate pamphlet. The whole book made up of *The Lovers of Gudrun* and the *Tributes* was issued in red, in blue, and in green cloth, watered-silk-grained, blocked on the recto cover with the name of the poem in large ornamental gilt letters and a design representing a boy bestriding the globe and blowing bubbles. The title is also lettered on the back, above two lighted torches, crossed. The edges are only moderately trimmed—not ploughed level all round. The endpapers are brown.

When Messrs. Roberts hit upon the device of separating *The Lovers of Gudrun* from *The Earthly Paradise* for the benefit of tourists, they little thought how distinguished a tourist (and on what an unusual tour) they were about to aid and abet in the operation of carrying coals to Newcastle. The little pocket volume was ready before Morris started on his first trip to Iceland. He knew that he would be obliged to accept hospitality at many a " stead " in lieu of hostel, and that it would be impossible to tender money for the refreshment he would get. He therefore took with him for a gift to Icelanders his version of their own Laxdæla Saga as printed and bound in Boston, Massachusetts ; and with these Anglo-American coals brought back to their native Newcastle those good folk were greatly pleased.

Before the concluding volume of *The Earthly Paradise* came out, another book resulting from the author's Icelandic studies was published. Its title-page reads thus :—

"*That spring was she just come to her full height,*
Low-bosomed yet she was, and slim and light,
Yet scarce might she grow fairer from that day;
Gold were the locks wherewith the wind did play,
Finer than silk, waved softly like the sea
After a three days' calm, and to her knee
Wellnigh they reached; fair were the white hands laid
Upon the door-posts where the dragons played."

FRONTISPIECE TO THE BOSTON (MASS.) "LOVERS OF GUDRUN."

(28)

VÖLSUNGA SAGA.

THE STORY

OF THE

VOLSUNGS & NIBLUNGS

WITH CERTAIN SONGS

FROM THE

ELDER EDDA.

TRANSLATED FROM THE ICELANDIC

BY

EIRÍKR MAGNÚSSON,

TRANSLATOR OF 'LEGENDS OF ICELAND;'

AND

WILLIAM MORRIS,

AUTHOR OF 'THE EARTHLY PARADISE.'

LONDON:

F. S. ELLIS, KING STREET, COVENT GARDEN.

MDCCCLXX.

There were only 750 copies of *Völsunga* printed. This again was a crown 8vo. uniform in size and style with *Grettir the Strong*. There are ten preliminary leaves, 275 pages of the book proper, and four pages of advertizements. The half-title ("*THE STORY OF THE VOLSUNGS.*") and title, each with blank verso, are followed by a Preface (pages v to xi : xii is blank), "Contents" (pages xiii to xvi), "The Names of those who are most noteworthy in this Story" (pages xvii and xviii), and "A Prologue in Verse" (pages xix and xx), consisting of six seven-line stanzas signed "William Morris." *The Story of the Volsungs and Niblungs* extends to page 163 (164 is blank) ; the headlines, in Italic capitals, are, versos, "*THE STORY OF THE*," rectos, "*VOLSUNGS AND NIBLUNGS.*" Page 165 is a half-title, "CERTAIN SONGS/ FROM/ THE ELDER EDDA,/ WHICH DEAL WITH THE STORY OF THE VOLSUNGS." The verso is blank. The Songs from the Edda occupy pages 167 to 270. The verso headlines are "*SONGS FROM THE EDDA.*" The recto headlines are the names of the particular songs, as "*THE LAY OF HELGI.*" Pages 271 and 272 contain notes,—pages 273 to 275 "An Alphabetical List of Persons, Places, and Things in the Story." At the foot of page 275 is the imprint " LONDON :/ STRANGEWAYS & WALDEN, Printers, 28 Castle Street, Leicester Square." The book was issued in a peculiarly fine green cloth, stamped in gold all over the sides and back from a most beautiful design by Morris. The end-papers are white.

Twelve certificated copies were printed on Whatman's hand-made paper of demy 8vo. size, and put up in blue paper boards with white backs ; and twelve more were printed on Whatman's hand-made paper of crown 8vo. size. These (which have no certificates) are very choice books if properly treated by a binder who had virgin quires to deal with and took care of all the deckel edges ; but some copies suffered a little by being put up in green cloth just like the ordinary copies. Why those beautiful covers, admirably executed by Messrs. Burn and Co., should have hurt the books, needs a word of explanation. The fact is that the hand-made paper is appreciably larger than the machine-made ; and to get the sheets within Morris's unmargined design necessitates a little trimming of deckel edges. A cheap popular edition was issued in the Camelot Series in 1888, with the following title :

(29)

VÖLSUNGA SAGA : THE STORY OF/ THE VOLSUNGS AND NIBLUNGS,/ WITH CERTAIN SONGS FROM/ THE ELDER EDDA. EDITED, WITH/ INTRODUC-TION AND NOTES, BY/ H. HALLIDAY SPARLING./ TRANSLATED FROM THE ICELANDIC, BY EIRÍKR/ MAG-NÚSSON (TRANSLATOR OF "LEGENDS OF/ ICELAND"); AND WILLIAM MORRIS (AUTHOR OF/ "THE EARTHLY PARADISE")./ WALTER SCOTT/ LONDON : 24 WAR-WICK LANE/ PATERNOSTER ROW/ 1888

The volume consists of preliminary pages i to lii, and text, index &c. 1 to 276.

The original edition of *The Story of the Volsungs and Niblungs* was through the press by April 1870 and came out soon after, when the second volume (Part III) of *The Earthly Paradise* was in its second edition. The first page of the advertizements in *Völsunga* offers the fifth editions of Parts I and II, and the second of Part III, and announces that "In October will be published the Fourth and concluding portion of *The Earthly Paradise.*" I do not think it was really ready much before December; but at all events it was out well before Christmas, with the following title :—

(30)

THE

EARTHLY PARADISE

A POEM.

BY

WILLIAM MORRIS,

AUTHOR OF THE LIFE AND DEATH OF JASON.

PART IV.

London : F. S. ELLIS, 33 *King Street, Covent Garden.*

MDCCCLXX.

This volume is as nearly as possible uniform with Part III. The half-title reads simply "THE EARTHLY PARADISE." The imprint at the back of the title-page is "LONDON :/ STRANGEWAYS AND WALDEN, PRINTERS,/ Castle St. Leicester Sq."/ The verso of the "Contents" is blank. And the text

5

begins at page 2 on the verso of a half-title reading "THE/ EARTHLY PARADISE./ DECEMBER, JANUARY,/ FEBRUARY." There are 442 pages of text—the last five being occupied by "L'Envoy," set in italics. At the end of page 442 is the imprint "LONDON :/ Printed by STRANGE-WAYS AND WALDEN, Castle St. Leicester Sq." The usual *Earthly Paradise* book-mark follows, with a blank verso ; and there are eight pages of Mr. Ellis's advertizements, three pages of which are notices of D. G. Rossetti's Poems, while four deal with Morris's works and the remaining one with Sir John Maundevile and Christina Rossetti's *Commonplace and other Stories.* The table of contents is as follows :—

CONTENTS.

In the advertizement of the completed *Earthly Paradise* it is stated that "Purchasers of Parts I. and II. in 1 vol. (as originally issued) will find a new title-page for that volume in Part IV." This new title was printed on thin wove paper like that of the original volume instead of the thickish laid paper employed for Parts III and IV ; and a new label was issued with it, reading "THE/ EARTHLY/ PARADISE./ W. MORRIS./ I. & II." How it was arranged for the copies containing the new title-page and label to get into the hands of purchasers of the original volume of 1868, I was never able to fathom. I have met with very few copies of Part IV containing the extra title and label, and have never seen a copy of the 1868 volume with the new title inserted and the new label affixed. The special title-page is as follows :—

THE
EARTHLY PARADISE

A POEM.

BY
WILLIAM MORRIS,
AUTHOR OF 'THE LIFE AND DEATH OF JASON.'

PARTS I. & II.

London: F. S. ELLIS, 33 *King Street, Covent Garden.*

MDCCCLXX.

[*All Rights reserved.*]

In my own set, the extra title and label of course still form part of the last volume of Part IV.

The large-paper copies of Part IV, again, were divided into two volumes, of which the first has three half-titles and a title before the poetry begins, for in addition to what is already described there is a leaf bearing the words "THE EARTHLY PARADISE./ Vol. V." That volume ends at page 230, three leaves being simply cut off sheet Q and pasted on to sheet P, while, to make Vol. VI ship-shape, a single leaf with a half-title like that of Vol. II is put with the remaining five leaves of sheet Q in front of sheet R. The labels are of course marked " V " and " VI."

It is worth recording, as one of the marks of genuineness, that the labels of Vol. III and Vol. IV (large paper), being on the model of those for Vol. I and Vol. II, do not fit the thinner measure, but have the first and last letters on the sides instead of the back. The labels for Vol. V and Vol. VI were therefore printed on the model of those for the ordinary copies of the second and third instalments, with the title in three lines instead of two.

This first edition of *The Earthly Paradise*, though marked by those opportunist features which have been noted, is a very nice book even on small paper. On large, it is distinctly choice and treasurable, for all its make-shiftness, if such a make-shift word may be used.

Of the first edition of Part IV, 1500 ordinary copies were printed. Whether any were converted into second edition copies I do not know; but 500 more were got from (31–32) the printer in December for the purposes of a second edition; and 1500 more in January 1871. The third edition is dated 1871 on the title and label.

A brief account of changes in the form of *The Earthly Paradise* must be added. In 1872 the publishers extended the popularity of the book by issuing it in monthly parts printed from the stereotyped plates of the original library issue, but with less margin. There were ten portable little volumes in limp cloth of the usual fine dark green colour, gilt-lettered at the back and on the front cover. The back-lettering is "THE/ EARTHLY/ PARADISE/ W. MORRIS/ I " [" II," " III," and so on]. On the front cover each part has the legend " THE/ EARTHLY PARADISE " at the top, and at the foot, in italic capitals, the names of the particular stories in the part. The title-pages, which are without the book-mark of other editions, read alike save in the lines, above the publishers' imprint, describing the contents of the particular part, and save that in Parts IX and X there are two changes in that imprint. In Part I the title reads thus—

(33)

THE/ EARTHLY PARADISE/ A POEM./ BY/ WILLIAM MORRIS,/ AUTHOR OF THE LIFE AND DEATH OF JASON./ POPULAR EDITION./ IN TEN PARTS./ *PART I./* PROLOGUE—THE WANDERERS./ ATALANTA'S RACE./ LONDON :/ ELLIS AND GREEN,/ 33 KING STREET, COVENT GARDEN, W.C./ MDCCCLXXII./ [*All Rights reserved.*]

The part contains pages 1 to 136 of Vol. I, with four preliminary leaves, namely a half-title with the book-mark on the
verso so as to form a frontispiece, the title, the dedication, and
the Contents of Vol. I, and four pages of advertizements at
the end.

The lines on the title special to Part II are *"PART II./*
THE MAN BORN TO BE KING./ THE DOOM OF
KING ACRISIUS./ THE PROUD KING." It has a half-
title with the book-mark on the verso, title, pages 137 to 343
of Vol. I, book-mark on verso of page 343, and four pages of
advertizements.

Part III has merely a title and the "Contents of Vol. II,"
pages 1 to 160 of that volume, and four pages of advertize-
ments. The distinctive lines of the title are *"PART III./*
THE STORY OF CUPID AND PSYCHE./ THE
WRITING ON THE IMAGE./ THE LOVE OF
ALCESTIS."

Part IV consists of pages 161 to 334 of Vol. II, without
advertizements, but just the usual title, with the distinctive
lines *"PART IV./* THE LADY OF THE LAND./ THE
SON OF CRŒSUS./ THE WATCHING OF THE
FALCON./ PYGMALION AND THE IMAGE./ OGIER
THE DANE."

In Part V pages 1 to 160 of Vol. III are put up with a title
and the "Contents" of the volume, and four pages of advertizements at the end. The distinctive lines are *"PART V./*
THE DEATH OF PARIS./ THE LAND EAST OF THE
SUN AND WEST OF/ THE MOON."

In Part VI a blank leaf and the title are pasted on before
pages 161 to 336, which is followed by four pages of adver-
tizements. The special lines of this title are *"PART
VI./* ACONTIUS AND CYDIPPE./ THE MAN WHO
NEVER LAUGHED AGAIN./ THE STORY OF
RHODOPE."

Part VII finishes up Vol. III. It is merely pages 337 to
526 with the title, a single leaf, pasted to page 337, and bearing the special lines *"PART VII./* THE LOVERS OF
GUDRUN."

Into Part VIII, which consists of pages 1 to 176 of Vol. IV,
are pasted the title and "Contents," and four pages of advertizements at the end. The distinctive lines of the title are

"*PART VIII.*/ THE GOLDEN APPLES./ THE FOSTER-ING OF ASLAUG./ BELLEROPHON AT ARGOS."

Part IX starts once more with a half-title, not uniform with previous ones, and a title which has the fresh imprint "LONDON :/ ELLIS AND GREEN,/ 29 NEW BOND STREET, W./ (*Late 33 King Street, Covent Garden*)./ MDCCCLXXII." The special lines are "*PART IX.*/ THE RING GIVEN TO VENUS./ BELLEROPHON IN LYCIA." The part extends from page 177 to page 320 of Vol. IV. The effort of removal to the classic premises of Mr. Boone seems to have exhausted the ingenuity of the publishers in the matter of dividing these volumes into Parts; for not only is this Part the first to fail of completing a story, but actually ends with an uncompleted sentence.

Part X takes up the unfinished sentence with page 321 and ends the book at page 442. It has a half-title, as well as a title with the special lines "*PART X.*/ BELLEROPHON IN LYCIA./ THE HILL OF VENUS./ EPILOGUE. L'ENVOI." There is another new imprint,—recalling to memory that the circumstances in which these closing parts were brought forth had sadness in them, apart from pressure of removal. Mr. Green died suddenly, at an early age ; and Mr. Ellis was again alone in the publishing business. The imprint setting forth this fact is "LONDON :/ F. S. ELLIS, 29 NEW BOND STREET, W./ (*Late 33 King Street, Covent Garden*)./ MDCCCLXXII." On a spare leaf at the end, Morris's pretty book-mark is given again ; but there are no advertizements.

All the title-pages alike have at the foot of the verso the imprint "LONDON :/ PRINTED BY JOHN STRANGEWAYS,/ Castle St. Leicester Sq." The scheme of publication was to get these charming little pocket volumes into the hands of the trade with the monthly magazines during ten months of the year 1872. No. I came out thus at the end of January with the February magazines, and so on till No. X appeared at the end of November with the December magazines. There was no part issued in October for November. Generally speaking each part had pasted to the first end-paper a 16mo. hand-bill giving notice when the next part would appear. These bills were headed "POPULAR EDITION,/ IN TEN MONTHLY PARTS/, OF/ MR. MORRIS'S GREAT POEM,/ THE

EARTHLY PARADISE/ *Containing Twenty-five Tales in Verse.*" The parts were offered at 3s. 6d. each (i.e. 2s. 8d. nett); and the bills ended with the address of the publishers. In the last part (VIII) which had the King Street address on its title the New Bond Street address appeared on the hand-bill. Of Parts I and II, 2000 copies were printed; of Part III, 1250; of each of the others, 1000. The popular edition received

(34)   a new form in 1886, when it was re-issued in five volumes instead of ten parts, on the transfer of the poet's works to Messrs. Reeves and Turner after Mr. Ellis's retirement from business.

In 1890 *The Earthly Paradise* was revised and printed in a single 8vo. volume, set in small type in double columns, 57 lines to the normal column. There is a half-title ("THE EARTHLY PARADISE.") with an imprint on the verso, "𝔅𝔞𝔩𝔩𝔞𝔫𝔱𝔶𝔫𝔢 𝔓𝔯𝔢𝔰𝔰/ BALLANTYNE, HANSON AND CO./ EDIN-BURGH AND LONDON." The title-page is

(35)

THE/ EARTHLY PARADISE/ A POEM/ BY/ WILLIAM MORRIS/ [Morris's book-mark—the debased rendering]/ LONDON/ REEVES AND TURNER, 196 STRAND/ 1890

on the verso of which are two lines of history—

FIRST EDITION, crown 8vo, 4 vols. 1868-70.

POPULAR EDITION, 10 parts, 12mo, 1872; and 5 vols. 12mo, 1886.

The Dedication with blank verso and "Contents" of two pages complete the preliminary half-sheet. The prologue occupies page 1; page 2 is blank; and the work proceeds in a plain (not to say ugly) business-like manner from page 3 to page 445, at the foot of which is the imprint "PRINTED BY BALLANTYNE, HANSON AND CO./ EDINBURGH AND LONDON": page 446 is blank; and a blank leaf completes the sheet. The book is unpleasant to look at, within; but the cover which the poet specially designed for it is very elegant. This was executed in cloth of three different colours,—olive, red, and white. Conventional sprigs of myrtle are stamped in gold round a more conventional centre ornament on the recto cover and blind on the verso. The back is a fine scroll design of bay with tulips interspersed; and the lettering is "THE/ EARTHLY/ PARADISE/ BY/ WILLIAM/ MORRIS/ LONDON/ 1891": it was not executed by Messrs. Burn & Co.; and the tone of the cloth did not come up to a high enough standard to do justice to the design. The end-papers are white; and a single leaf of advertizements is generally found pasted before the half-title.

However, here was a revised text and one more fine piece of cloth blocking so far as design goes; and this revised text was all ready for the sumptuous Kelmscott edition, which was still being printed when the poet died. This final edition is in eight 8vo. volumes, printed in the golden type, in black and red. The size is something between a demy and a royal, but squarer. The titles, colophons, and component parts are as follows:

(36)

THE EARTHLY PARADISE. BY WILLIAM/ MORRIS. VOLUME I. PROLOGUE: THE/ WANDERERS. MARCH: ATALANTA'S/ RACE. THE MAN BORN TO BE KING.

This title is on the recto of the second leaf in Sig. a (the first is blank but for the signature, a1). On the verso of the title the old dedication is printed in one line, at the head, TO MY WIFE I DEDICATE THIS BOOK. The third leaf, recto and verso, is occupied by the Apology. Of the fourth the recto is blank and the verso filled by an ornamental border within which are a special decorative heading for the Prologue, and the Argument of the same in golden type capitals. The counterpart border faces, on what counts as page 1; and the Prologue is started in capitals, according to Kelmscott wont. There are two more pairs of ornamental borders for *Atalanta's Race* and *The Man born to be King;* and the volume ends on page 193 with the short colophon "Printed by William Morris at the Kelmscott Press,/ and finished on the 7th day of May, 1896." There are three blank leaves completing the half sheet on the first leaf of which the poem closes; and the end-papers consist of four leaves (half a sheet) at each end, including the paste-down. The title of Vol. II is printed on the fourth leaf of a half-sheet whereof the first three are blank. The words are

THE EARTHLY PARADISE. BY WILLIAM/ MORRIS. VOLUME II. APRIL: THE/ DOOM OF KING ACRISIUS. THE PROUD/ KING. .

There are 121 pages, including two pairs of ornamental borders for the two tales ; and the colophon reads " Printed by William Morris at the Kelmscott Press,/ and finished on the 24th day of June, 1896." This is on the fifth of six leaves forming the last signature : the sixth is blank. The end-papers are half-sheets. Of Vol. III again the title is on the fourth leaf of a half-sheet, the other three being blank : it is

THE EARTHLY PARADISE. BY WILLIAM/ MORRIS. VOLUME III. MAY: THE STORY/ OF CUPID AND PSYCHE. THE WRITING/ ON THE IMAGE. JUNE: THE LOVE OF/ ALCESTIS. THE LADY OF THE LAND.

The 169 pages which follow include of course four pairs of borders this time. The last signature has again six leaves, the last blank, and the recto of the last but one, page 169, closing with the colophon " Printed by William Morris at the Kelmscott Press,/ and finished on the 24th day of August, 1896." The end-papers are half-sheets. The title-page following the three blank leaves of the first half-sheet in the next volume reads thus :

THE EARTHLY PARADISE. BY WILLIAM/ MORRIS. VOLUME IV. JULY: THE SON/ OF CRŒSUS. THE WATCHING OF THE/ FALCON. AUGUST : PYGMALION AND/ THE IMAGE. OGIER THE DANE.

Here again, as there are four tales, there are four pairs of lovely borders. The last signature has six leaves—one blank : on the recto of the fifth, page 137, the text ends, and is followed by the sadly changed colophon " Printed by the Trustees of the late William Morris at/ the Kelmscott Press, and finished on the 25th day of/ November, 1896." The end-papers are half-sheets. The fifth volume also starts with a half-sheet bearing not a mark save the following title on the fourth leaf:

THE EARTHLY PARADISE. BY WILLIAM/ MORRIS. VOLUME V. SEPTEMBER :/ THE DEATH OF PARIS. THE LAND EAST/ OF THE SUN AND WEST OF THE MOON./ OCTOBER: THE STORY OF ACONTIUS/ AND CYDIPPE. THE MAN WHO NEVER/ LAUGHED AGAIN.

There are four pairs of borders for the four tales; the last page (241) is printed on the first leaf of a half-sheet so as to leave three blank leaves beside the usual four-leaf end-papers; and the Trustees' imprint sets forth that the book was finished on Christmas-eve 1896. The title of the sixth volume follows the usual allowance of blank leaves, and is

THE EARTHLY PARADISE. BY WILLIAM/ MORRIS. VOLUME VI. NOVEMBER :/ THE STORY OF RHODOPE. THE LOVERS/ OF GUDRUN.

The volume contains 217 pages, including two pairs of ornamental borders, and was finished on the 18th of February, 1897.

The seventh volume has the following title :—

THE EARTHLY PARADISE. BY WILLIAM/ MORRIS VOLUME VII. DECEMBER :/ THE GOLDEN APPLES. THE FOSTERING/ OF ASLAUG. JANUARY: BELLEROPHON/ AT ARGOS. THE RING GIVEN TO VENUS.

Here the 203 pages include four pairs of borders. The printing, according to the Trustees' colophon, was finished on the 17th of March, 1897.

In the eighth volume the title reads thus :

THE EARTHLY PARADISE. BY WILLIAM/ MORRIS. VOLUME VIII. FEBRUARY :/ BELLEROPHON IN LYCIA. THE HILL OF/ VENUS. EPILOGUE. L'ENVOI.

The 186 pages include two pairs of borders ; and the colophon of the Trustees gives the 10th of June, 1897, as the date on which the printing of the whole book was completed.

The volumes of the Kelmscott *Earthly Paradise* are bound by Leighton in the usual style in limp vellum with silk ties and gilt lettering across the back worded thus—" THE/ EARTHLY/ PARADISE/ BY/ WILLIAM/ MORRIS/ VOL. I " [" II " and so on]. On the first volume this legend is in bold type: in the second, a thin volume, the size of type had to be reduced; and the smaller size is used in the rest whether thick or thin. In the matter of lavish blank leaves and end-papers the volumes are practically uniform.

HORRINGTON HOUSE

LOVE IS ENOUGH
MORE SAGAS—THE ÆNEIDS OF VIRGIL
THE TWO SIDES OF THE RIVER &c.
THE STORY OF SIGURD THE VOLSUNG

HORRINGTON HOUSE:

LOVE IS ENOUGH—THE ÆNEIDS OF VIRGIL—THE TWO SIDES OF THE RIVER &C.—THE STORY OF SIGURD THE VOLSUNG AND THE FALL OF THE NIBLUNGS.

Delightful as Morris has made the old-world stories which are the substance of *The Life and Death of Jason* and *The Earthly Paradise*, there were still lands for him to conquer. In those books we see the result of his long session at the feet of Chaucer. In the next group there are higher spiritual qualities, and more artistic inventiveness, and a more virile handling, especially in *Sigurd the Volsung*. To go on with our annals,—soon after the completion of *The Earthly Paradise* a short poem entitled *The Dark Wood* was placed in Mr. Morley's hands: it appeared in *The Fortnightly Review* for February 1871. By this time Morris had completed, or nearly completed, his fine rendering of the legendary Saga of Frithiof the Bold, on which Bishop Esaias Tegnér's ornate modern poem of that name is founded. Morris's version of the Saga appeared, with his name alone as translator, in *The Dark Blue Magazine* for March and April 1871. Of the next volume of original poetry, through the press of November 1872, the title is—

(37)

LOVE IS ENOUGH

OR

THE FREEING OF PHARAMOND

A MORALITY.

BY

WILLIAM MORRIS.

LONDON:

ELLIS & WHITE, 29 NEW BOND STREET.

1873.

This book,—which, by the way, so keen a critic as the late Coventry Patmore more than once named to me in conversation as, in his opinion, Morris's masterpiece,—was printed in a size not used before for Morris's works. Many of the verses being very long, the sightliness of the ordinary crown 8vo. page would have been marred by the constant need for turned lines. A size described as square crown 8vo. was therefore adopted: the height is that of ordinary crown 8vo., the width about half an inch greater. The size is in fact got by using an imperial paper and folding it in sixteen; so that imperial 16mo. is the correct term. The paper in this case is a wove paper of moderate substance and of a warm creamy tone. The poem occupies 134 pages: there are four preliminary leaves and a final leaf with advertizements on both sides. The first leaf is blank; the half-title, reading " LOVE IS ENOUGH," has a blank verso; the title has at the foot of the verso an imprint, " LONDON :/ PRINTED BY JOHN STRANGEWAYS,/ Castle St. Leicester Sq."; and the fourth leaf has a list of *dramatis personæ* on the recto, the verso being blank. The pages of the poem are numbered with Arabic figures in the outer top corners ; and the head-lines, recto and verso, are "*LOVE IS ENOUGH*" in italic capitals. The cover (with white end-papers) is of a beautiful dark green cloth like that of *Völsunga*. The only blocking is a broad band (two inches) of interlaced willow and flowering myrtle stamped in gold, with the legend "Love is Enough" finely drawn amid the leaves : the same legend is stamped boldly in gold up the back. The binding was so admirably executed by Messrs. Burn and Co. that, like *Völsunga*, *Love is Enough* perfectly well preserved in the original cover is a really treasurable thing. The number of copies printed was 1500.

Twenty-five copies of *Love is Enough* were printed on Whatman's hand-made paper of demy 8vo. size and put up in "Turner grey" paper boards with cream-white backs,—the bands showing through the paper,—and printed labels reading simply " LOVE/ IS/ ENOUGH." Save in size, the only variations from the ordinary paper copies are the presence of a certificate on the verso of the fly-title—it might as well have been on the blank leaf—reading " *Twenty-five copies printed on large paper for/ Private Circulation only.*" As the book was set for a square-shaped page like a small quarto, the proportion of the top and bottom margins to the front has not the rectitude evident in the ordinary copies; and the desirableness of the large paper book rests upon the probable eternal durability of its paper and the mere scarcity and tallness. No sane book-collector would part with his Whatman copy; but then he must keep his ordinary copy too.

Beside the two issues of the first edition on paper, four copies were printed on fine writing vellum. They were very well done; though for my part I prefer the cheaper and thinner Roman vellum used in later years at the Kelmscott Press.

The sale of *Love is Enough* was never commensurate with the merits and beauties of the book; and the second edition was probably a portion of the original 1500 copies (38–39) but with a fresh title-page. There were copies transferred to Messrs. Reeves and Turner when Mr. Ellis left business; and a third edition was made from quire stock still existing in 1889. The half-title and title were reprinted on thin paper and inserted between the original blank leaf and list of *dramatis personæ*. Some of these 1889 copies were still to be had of Messrs. Longmans a short time since; but their current issue of *Love is Enough* is in one book with *Poems by the Way*.

The next book was to some extent a work of clearing up,— being in great part a revised reprint from *The Fortnightly* and *Dark Blue*. The title is—

(40)

THREE NORTHERN

LOVE STORIES,

AND OTHER TALES.

TRANSLATED FROM THE ICELANDIC

BY

EIRÍKR MAGNUSSON AND WILLIAM MORRIS.

———

LONDON:

ELLIS & WHITE, 29 NEW BOND STREET.

1875.

6

The edition of 500 copies was printed by June 1875. This is a crown 8vo. volume uniform with *Grettir* and *Völsunga*. The half-title reads " THREE/ NORTHERN LOVE STORIES,/ AND OTHER TALES." This and the title have blank versos; the Preface occupies pages v to viii; viii is blank; ix and xi are a " chronology " for *Gunnlaug* and a " Contents " for the whole book, each with a blank verso. A fresh half-title follows, reading " THE STORY OF/ GUNN-LAUG THE WORM-TONGUE/ AND RAVEN THE SKALD." The text of the Stories begins on page 3 and ends on page 243,—each tale having its half-title with blank verso, namely " THE STORY OF/ FRITHIOF THE BOLD," " THE STORY OF/ VIGLUND THE FAIR," " THE TALE OF/ HOGNI AND HEDINN," " THE TALE OF/ ROI THE FOOL," and " THE TALE OF/ THORSTEIN STAFF-SMITTEN ": pages 245 to 256 contain notes and indexes. At the foot of the last is the imprint " LONDON :/ PRINTED BY JOHN STRANGEWAYS, Castle St. Leicester Sq." The verso head-lines read *" THE STORY OF "* or *" THE TALE OF,"*— the rectos *" GUNNLAUG THE WORM-TONGUE," " HOGNI AND HEDINN,"* and so on, in Italic capitals. Page vii originally had a misprint, a distinctive Icelandic letter signifying *th* was given as a p, twice over. For this a cancel-leaf was printed. In some copies the original leaf remains with the cancel. The book was issued in the customary cloth of " Morris green," unblocked, with a printed back-label reading " THREE/ NORTHERN/ LOVE/ STORIES,/ AND/ OTHER TALES./ E. MAGNÚSSON/ AND/ W. MORRIS./ 10s. 6d."

There were twenty-five copies printed on Whatman's hand-made paper, demy 8vo., without other variations from the ordinary copies, save that, if pages vii-viii are a cancel-leaf, the half-title also is, as they are connected. These copies were put up in blue paper boards with white backs, rounded, but the bands showing through the paper. The printed label reads " THREE/ NORTHERN/ LOVE/ STORIES/ AND OTHER TALES."

Morris had been at work on this book as far back as the winter of 1873, when he mentioned to me in a letter returning a copy of George Stevenson's *Frithiof* which I had borrowed for him, that he should add *Viglund the Fair* to the already published *Gunnlaug* and *Frithiof*, together with three other tales "to make up," as he said, "a book big enough for Ellis's purposes." In a later letter of the same winter he told me of the final selection of *Hroi the Fool, Hogni and Hedin,* and *Thorstein Staff-smitten.* Of these titles the spelling was altered a little for the book. One of the tales, that of Thorstein, he described to me as "simple and not without generosity, smelling strong of the soil of Iceland like the Gunnlaug." At this time (December 1873), Morris was living, not any longer at Queen's Square where we had last met, but "down Turnham Green way opposite Chiswick Lane." The house was called Horrington House; and it was there, very shortly afterwards, that he showed me a beautiful manuscript which he had made of his then recent translation of the Eyrbyggja Saga. After reading passages of it to me, he told me that this Saga-writing and Saga-printing was practically a luxury he allowed himself, as he had still but few "converts to Sagaism," and the reading public cared little about the works. He therefore did much of his translating from the Icelandic as a Sunday amusement; and the charming caligraphy of the *Eyrbyggja* he called his "Sunday writing."

It is worth noting, in the matter of the *Three Northern Love Stories,* that although *Frithiof* had appeared in the *Dark Blue* with only Morris's name as translator, the book does not discriminate in any way between that and the rest as regards the joint responsibility for the translation.

It was in the Summer of 1875 that the *Northern Love Stories* came out. The next work was also one of translation, but without a collaborator,—the Virgil. I remember well falling in with the stalwart poet in the Aldersgate Street Station of the Underground Railway, and travelling a little way with him. On the journey to Baker Street he showed me a quarto stiff-covered copy-book such as he used for his first drafts. This contained the portion of the *Æneid* which he was then writing; and he told me he did much of it in the train. I had read for him the proofs of the third part of *The Earthly Paradise,* to look after matters of a more or less mechanical kind; and it was agreed that I was to have the pleasure of doing the same for the Virgil. The last proofs were read by the beginning of October, and before the month was out I had my copy of the completed book of which the title-page is as follows:

6—2

(41)

THE

ÆNEIDS OF VIRGIL

DONE INTO ENGLISH VERSE

BY

WILLIAM MORRIS,

AUTHOR OF 'THE EARTHLY PARADISE.'

LONDON:

ELLIS AND WHITE, NEW BOND STREET.

MDCCCLXXVI.

Being written in the ballad metre of Chapman's Homer's Iliad, this book had to be, for the sake of sightliness, wide enough to take the line unturned. Hence there was a second " square crown 8vo." (Imperial 16mo.) like *Love is Enough*, but nearly thrice as thick. This time, laid paper like that of most of the books issued from King Street and New Bond Street had been obtained. The poem occupies 382 pages. It is preceded by two leaves and followed by a single blank leaf. The first leaf, the half-title, reads "THE/ ÆNEIDS OF VIRGIL"; and the verso is blank. On the verso of the title-page, at the foot, is the usual imprint, "LONDON :/ PRINTED BY JOHN STRANGEWAYS,/ Castle St. Leicester Sq." The paging is of the usual kind ; and the head-lines, in Roman capitals, verso "THE ÆNEIDS OF VIRGIL," recto " BOOK I " and so on. At the foot of page 382 is the imprint of Strangeways again but in two lines instead of three. The book was put up in the usual " Morris-green " cloth, unblocked, with a printed back-label reading "THE/ ÆNEIDS/ OF VIRGIL./ W. MORRIS./ 14s." The edition consisted of 1000 copies.

Twenty-five copies were printed on Whatman's hand-made paper of demy 8vo. size with no variation from the ordinary copies so far as the body of the book is concerned, except in the matter of margins. The paging is continuous, of course ; and when it was decided to put the sheets up in two thin volumes instead of one thick one, separate half-titles and titles were printed—like the ordinary ones, but with the additional line above the publisher's imprint, " BOOKS I—VI " and

" BOOKS VII—XII." To get the division right, the sheet signed N, which contains the end of Book VI and the beginning of Book VII, was cut in two down the back fold and "overcast" in the binding. The volumes were put up in Turner grey paper boards with almost flat cream-white backs (the bands showing through the paper), and printed labels reading " THE/ ÆNEIDS/ OF/ VIRGIL./ Books I—VI. [VII—XII.]/ W. MORRIS." These large-paper copies are extremely well produced ; but they are of course open to the exception taken at page 81 to a naturally square-paged book printed on tall but not wide paper.

By the winter of 1875-6 Morris must, I think, have been in full swing with his great poem *Sigurd the Volsung*,—perhaps the greatest of all his works. Whether at this time he was much worried for contributions of verse to periodicals, I cannot positively say ; but I fancy he had to decline many proposals of that kind. Be that as it may, it is certain that he supplied the editor of *The Athenæum* in the spring of 1876 with a bright little reminiscence of the *Earthly Paradise* period. In that journal for the 13th of May 1876 appeared *The First Foray of Aristomenes*, described as " a fragment of a poem called *The Story of Aristomenes*." It is written in the Chaucerian heroic couplets which he so much affected in earlier years. He has never gathered it into his published works ; but it has a permanent form in a thin privately printed pamphlet—

(42) ⌢

THE TWO SIDES OF
THE RIVER
HAPLESS LOVE
AND
THE FIRST FORAY OF
ARISTOMENES
BY
WILLIAM MORRIS

LONDON
1876
[*Not for Sale*]

Of this thin crown 8vo., which, for the rest, looks much like the spilth of that project for enlarging the *Guenevere* volume when reprinting it the year before, the half-title is "THE TWO SIDES OF THE RIVER/ HAPLESS LOVE/ AND/ THE FIRST FORAY OF/ ARISTOMENES." The verso is blank : so is that of the title-page given above. The three poems occupy pages 5 to 22; and there is a blank leaf at the end. The title of each poem is used as head-line (in italic capitals, recto and verso); and in all respects the printing and paper are like those of the other Morris crown octavos of that period. In the few copies which I have seen the pamphlet is sewn into a printed wrapper on the front of which the legend of the half-title is reproduced within a border of thin rules, thus—

THE TWO SIDES OF THE RIVER

HAPLESS LOVE

AND

THE FIRST FORAY OF

ARISTOMENES

This wrapper is of a pale sage-green colour, thin, and somewhat shiny ; and it is accompanied in copies which I have seen by a leaf of thin white paper at each end, presumably to avoid the contrast between the creamy paper of the book and the green of the wrapper.

It may be fairly supposed that, if the *Guenevere* reprint had contained additional poems, not theretofore collected, these would have included *The Two Sides of the River* and *Hapless Love.* There might also have been *The God of the Poor, On the Edge of the Wilderness*, and *The Dark Wood ;* and it seems a pity that this charming little private print did not contain six poems instead of three. However, those three, omitted from the pamphlet, were gathered into the *Poems by the Way* in the Kelmscott Press days later on; and, curiously, two out of the three in the pamphlet were then left out in the cold,—*Hapless Love* and the *Aristomenes* fragment.

In the winter of 1876 came out *Sigurd the Volsung*, dated 1877. I had my copy by the 20th of November 1876. The title-page reads—

(43)

THE STORY

OF

SIGURD THE VOLSUNG,

AND THE

FALL OF THE NIBLUNGS.

BY

WILLIAM MORRIS,

AUTHOR OF 'THE EARTHLY PARADISE.'

LONDON :

ELLIS AND WHITE, NEW BOND STREET.

MDCCCLXXVII.

Being written in long lines, *Sigurd* had to be of the same square form as *Love is Enough* and the Virgil, in order to range with the other works. Square crown 8vo. (Imperial 16mo.) it accordingly was. The poem fills 392 pages; and there are four preliminary leaves,—a half-title ("THE STORY/ OF/ SIGURD THE VOLSUNG/ AND THE/ FALL OF THE NIBLUNGS") with a blank verso, the title with the three-line imprint at the foot of the verso,—"LONDON :/ PRINTED BY JOHN STRANGEWAYS,/ Castle St. Leicester Sq."—and three pages of "Contents." The paging is in Arabic figures as usual; and the head-lines, in roman capitals, are (verso) "THE STORY OF SIGURD THE VOLSUNG," (recto) "BOOK I. SIGMUND," and so on. This book again was done up in "Morris-green" cloth unblocked, with a printed back-label reading "THE STORY/ OF/ SIGURD/ THE VOLSUNG/ AND/ THE FALL OF THE/ NIBLUNGS./ W. MORRIS./ 12s." The edition consisted of 2500 copies; and on this occasion again there were twenty-five Whatman paper copies, demy 8vo., a size which, as in the case of the large-paper *Love is Enough* and Virgil, "becomes" the page of type less than the ordinary size does. The Whatman copies are done up in Turner-grey paper boards with a cream-white back and a printed label like the ordinary one but with the price omitted.

The original impression of *Sigurd* was still not quite exhausted when Mr. Ellis retired in 1885; but there were not very many copies to be transferred to Messrs. Reeves and Turner, who published a fresh edition in the summer of 1887. The 2500 copies printed ten years before must have (44–45) served for the second and third editions as well as the first; for this one of the new publishers is called the fourth. The title-page reads as follows:

(46)

THE STORY/ OF/ SIGURD THE VOLSUNG/ AND THE/ FALL OF THE NIBLUNGS./ BY/ WILLIAM MORRIS,/ AUTHOR OF 'THE EARTHLY PARADISE.'/ *FOURTH EDITION./* LONDON: REEVES AND TURNER, 196, STRAND./ MDCCCLXXXVII

Like the original issue, this has four preliminary leaves; but the body of the book is printed with thinner leads between the lines, and makes only 345 pages instead of 392. There are six pages of Reeves and Turner's advertizements at the end. The size of the book is imperial 16mo. again; but the large-paper copies, instead of being done in demy 8vo., were done in crown quarto on Dickenson's hand-made paper. They are handsome books, half-bound in vellum with cloth sides flowered all over in green and gold, and with printed back-labels reading "THE STORY/ OF/ SIGURD/ THE VOLSUNG/ AND/ THE FALL OF THE/ NIBLUNGS./ W. MORRIS." I am glad to think that there will be enough of these fine and durable volumes to "please the eyes of many men" in the coming century; for the number printed was, I believe, a hundred. Those men are not to have the sumptuous folio which the poet

designed to print at the Kelmscott Press; and very few of
them will ever hold in their hands the single sheet which the
Trustees caused to be pulled for presentation to the poet's
friends before distributing this noble combination of the Troy
type. Nothing can be sadder to those friends than this
uncompleted sheet, printed on one side only. On its first page,
within a border of grape-vine, is the opening of Book I,
" Sigmund," headed thus—

(47)

IN THIS BOOK IS TOLD OF THE EARLIER DAYS
OF THE VOL-/SUNGS AND OF SIGMUND THE
FATHER OF SIGURD, AND OF/ HIS DEEDS,
AND OF HOW HE DIED WHILE SIGURD WAS
YET/ UNBORN IN HIS MOTHER'S WOMB./ Of
the dwelling of King Volsung, and the wedding of Signy
his daughter.

Below this heading, for a space of 3½ inches, the right-hand
side is filled with the opening of the poem; while the left-
hand side is blank for lack of the large ornamental word
" There " which Morris was to design—

There was a dwelling of kings ere the world was waxen old

being the first line. Pages 2 and 3 of this sheet are blank;
and page 4 is numbered 16,—showing that the book was
meant to be gathered into fasciculi of four sheets for binding.
At the foot of this last page is printed in red the following
statement of the Trustees :—" Incomplete sheet of Sigurd the
Volsung. 32 copies printed at the Kelmscott Press on/
Jan. 11, 1897, before the distribution of the type. Not for
sale."

But although those men of next century will not have the
great folio *Sigurd* uniform with the Kelmscott Chaucer, there
is reason to hope they will have 160 copies on paper and six on
vellum of a small folio edition which the Trustees of the poet
announce. It is to be printed in the Chaucer type, in black
and red, with two wood-cuts designed by Sir Edward
(48) Burne-Jones, and new borders designed by the poet;
and I regret that I cannot describe it here, though giving it
a number as if it were an accomplished fact. I wonder whether

those next century men will think they would have preferred it in the Golden type. If so, they may fall back on the small pica of Strangeways on Dickenson's paper already described. I am harping on those men because it seems to me that their ancestors now present ambng us have not fully appreciated the might and magnitude of this epic. There are doubtless a few who regard it as among the great works of the age and indeed of English literature. Twenty years ago, when it was brand-new, it was my luck to meet the late Mathilde Blind and Mr. Theodore Watts (now Watts-Dunton) at the house of my dear old friend W. B. Scott. We were all full of *Sigurd;* and Miss Blind, with that fresh enthusiasm which distinguished her to the end, held staunchly that there was no English epic superior to it. "I think," she said in her broad German-English,—German only in the pronunciation, for she spoke and wrote the idiom perfectly,—"I think it is quaïte as good as Baradaïse Lost!" And for my part I am content to leave that question for those next-century fellows to settle.

KELMSCOTT HOUSE

LECTURES
LETTERS &c. ON PUBLIC QUESTIONS

Kelmscott House, Upper Mall,
Hammersmith, on a bright day
soon after the 3rd of October
1896 when William Morris
died there.

KELMSCOTT HOUSE:

We have now followed Morris through his books to the
end of the years during which he stood before the public as
an artist alone,—poet, designer, worker in all or most decorative crafts. By the time at which we have arrived, 1877, he
was interesting himself a good deal in public questions other
than artistic. His first notable utterance on such a question,
as far as I recollect, is a very striking letter to the Editor of
The Daily News. Written at 26 Queen Square, Bloomsbury,
on the 24th of October 1876, it appeared in the paper on the
26th, headed " England and the Turks," and was signed
" William Morris, Author of ' The Earthly Paradise.' "   On
the rumour of our going to war with Russia for the sake of
the Turks, the poet roundly denounced Lord Beaconsfield, and
called upon other quiet men, " sentimentalists " or what not,
to bestir themselves. His burden was " No war for thieves
and murderers "; and he kept it up for the best part of a
column. It was not surprising that he followed this up by
taking an active part in the work of the Eastern Question
Association, of which he became Treasurer. On Monday the
14th of May 1877 a meeting was held at Myddelton Hall,
Islington, to protest against any action of the Government
involving England in a war, the effect of which would have
been to maintain Turkish Tyranny. To this agitation Morris
contributed a poem of five eight-line stanzas printed on one
side of a single demy 8vo leaf, which was freely circulated
among the mechanics of London. It was headed

(49)

WAKE, LONDON LADS!
Air, The Hardy Norseman's home of yore.

and was signed in full, WILLIAM MORRIS. A placard

headed UNJUST WAR, which was posted about London at
 the same period, is attributed to Morris's pen;
(50-51) and of this copies were reprinted on a slip for
 hand to hand distribution. At about the same time
he was busy with others in founding the Society for the Protection of Ancient Buildings, familiarly known as " the Anti-
scrape Society," or more briefly " the Anti-scrape." The
manifesto of that body was written by him, and issued as an
ordinary prospectus on a sheet of post quarto writing paper,
four pages : those who wish may call the first page a title-page.
It was printed simultaneously in English and in French, the
first page consisting of the usual details as to the Society's
Officers &c., and the manifesto following on pages 2, 3, and 4.
The heading is, in the English version,

(52)

Society for the Protection of Ancient Buildings.

OFFICES :—9 BUCKINGHAM STREET, ADELPHI, LONDON, W.C.

and in the French version,

(53)

Société pour la Protection des Anciens Monuments.

BUREAUX :—9 BUCKINGHAM STREET, ADELPHI, LONDRES, W.C.

The list of honorary Secretaries, which follows three columns
of names of the Committee, opens in each version with

 William Morris, Kelmscott House, Hammersmith.

To that house he had lately moved from Hornington House,
Turnham Green ; and from there during the rest of his life
he issued a vast number of communications to the press in
furtherance of the aims of the " Anti-scrape." The Prospectus
has always been kept in print, varying as to the names of the
Committee and Officers, and also in form. At present it is
printed on a half-sheet post folio, two pages : The lower half of
the first contains the opening of the manifesto, headed thus :

(54 to 57)

[THE FOLLOWING ARE THE PRINCIPLES OF THE
 SOCIETY FOR/ THE PROTECTION OF ANCIENT
 BUILDINGS AS SET FORTH/ UPON ITS FOUN-
 DATION IN 1877, AND WHICH ARE HERE/
 REPRINTED IN 1896 WITHOUT ALTERATION.]

The second page ends with a list of Local Correspondents
which formed no part of the original print, though it occurs
on quarto reissues dated March 1882 and June 1885. The
folio half-sheet was adopted at least as long ago as 1891.
The Society has issued annual reports from the first. Of these
there are nineteen. It is safe to assume that Morris had to
do with most if not all of them ; but they are scarcely
to be numbered among his works. They are post 8vo.
pamphlets in grey wrappers. The title-page of the first is
—" 𝔖𝔬𝔠𝔦𝔢𝔱𝔶 𝔣𝔬𝔯 𝔱𝔥𝔢 𝔓𝔯𝔬𝔱𝔢𝔠𝔱𝔦𝔬𝔫/ 𝔬𝔣 𝔄𝔫𝔠𝔦𝔢𝔫𝔱 𝔅𝔲𝔦𝔩𝔡𝔦𝔫𝔤𝔰,/ The
First Annual Meeting of/ the Society./ Report of the
Committee/ thereat read./ 21st. June, 1878./ WILLIAM
MORRIS,/ *Hon. Sec.*" The rest do not often vary much from
that model, though the 7th mentions a paper and the 12th
an address by Morris. In 1881 a small 4to. volume of transactions was issued ; and there have been many printed circulars,
leaflets, and pamphlets. Those which were certainly written
by Morris will be mentioned in chronological order.

Morris soon got to be in demand as a public lecturer on
subjects connected with the arts ; nor was it long before the
social and political aspects of his themes took very serious
hold on him. In 1878 he published

(58)

THE DECORATIVE ARTS

THEIR RELATION TO

MODERN LIFE AND PROGRESS

AN ADDRESS

Delivered before the Trades' Guild of Learning

BY

WILLIAM MORRIS.

LONDON:

ELLIS AND WHITE,

29 NEW BOND STREET.

This crown 8vo. pamphlet, issued on the 4th of February 1878, consists of 32 pages including the title of which the verso is blank, and a Turner grey paper wrapper on which the title is repeated within a plain thin-rule border. It is paged in the ordinary way, has head-lines throughout ("*The Decorative Arts*"), and a one-line imprint at the foot of page 32, beneath a thin rule, "London : Printed by JOHN STRANGEWAYS, Castle St. Leicester Sq." Two thousand copies were printed ; and, as a rule, they were issued with the edges cut, and with no date; but I remember criticizing the pamphlet on both points on the day of its issue, and obtaining as a favour a copy or two uncut. Later on, the wrapper was reprinted with the date 1878 at foot. Cut copies so dated are rarer than cut copies undated. An uncut, dated copy, I never saw. The thing to have as representing the *editio princeps* is, of course, a copy undated and uncut.

A year later Morris was lecturing at Birmingham as President of the Birmingham Society of Arts and School of Design. His address was published as an 8vo. pamphlet (cut round the edges) with the following title-page :—

(59)

𝔅irmingham
𝔖ociety of 𝔄rts and 𝔖chool of 𝔇esign.

ADDRESS

DELIVERED IN

THE TOWN HALL, BIRMINGHAM,

ON THE 19TH OF FEBRUARY, 1879,

BY

WM. MORRIS, M.A.,
PRESIDENT.

BIRMINGHAM :
PRINTED BY E. C. OSBORNE, 84, NEW STREET.

The verso of this title-page is blank. The address occupies pages 3 to 23, the last having the printer's imprint repeated at foot, and a blank verso. There are no headlines; and the pages are numbered centrally in Arabic figures.

The year 1880 produced a second Birmingham presidential address, also printed as a pamphlet,—with the following title:—

(60)

BIRMINGHAM
SOCIETY OF ARTS & SCHOOL OF DESIGN.

———

LABOUR AND PLEASURE,
VERSUS
LABOUR AND SORROW.

AN

ADDRESS
BY
WILLIAM MORRIS, ESQ., M.A.,
PRESIDENT,
IN THE TOWN HALL, BIRMINGHAM,
19TH FEBRUARY, 1880.

BIRMINGHAM:
CUND BROS., PRINTERS, LONDON WORKS, MOOR STREET.

This pamphlet is an 8vo. with cut edges, carefully printed on a good toned paper. It is so imposed as to be folded but once and stitched through the crease. The title (in fancy letters) has a blank verso, and is followed by a half-title (lines 3 to 5 of the title) with a quotation from Defoe set in an italic colophon. The verso of this, also, is blank. The Address commences on what is really the fifth page but is counted as page 3; and it extends to page 31. Pages 4 to 31 are numbered centrally in Arabic figures, there being no head-lines. Page 32 is not numbered. In the centre, between two thin 2-em rules, is the imprint "BIRMINGHAM :/ CUND BROTHERS, PRINTERS, LONDON

7

WORKS, PATERNOSTER ROW,/ MOOR STREET." The last leaf is
blank. This pamphlet is very scarce. Unless perfectly clean,
it is somehow abnormally ugly, the type being small for an
8vo. page, and the margins ill proportioned. A copy in mint
state, however, has a look of attractiveness quite irresistible to
the collector. A circular about the Hammersmith carpets,
dated 24 May 1880 and issued by Morris and Co., was doubtless written by the poet himself ; but see the Appendix.

In 1881 he delivered an address at Burslem : it was printed
in an 8vo. pamphlet of which the following is the title-page :—

(61)

THE

WEDGWOOD INSTITUTE.

REPORTS

OF THE

Schools of Science & Art,

FOR THE YEAR

1880-81,

WITH THE

ADDRESS DELIVERED

BY

Mr. WILLIAM MORRIS,

at the Twelfth Annual Meeting,

HELD IN THE BURSLEM TOWN HALL,

OCTOBER 13th, 1881

Warwick Savage, Printer, Burslem.

The verso of the title is blank. The pamphlet is sewn and
cut, and has 28 pages. Morris's address begins on page 9 and
ends on page 23. The rest is occupied with reports, accounts,
lists, &c.

In 1882 he issued a collection of his lectures under the
general title,

(62)

HOPES AND FEARS
FOR ART.

FIVE LECTURES DELIVERED IN BIRMINGHAM, LONDON, AND NOTTINGHAM,

1878-1881.

BY

WILLIAM MORRIS,

AUTHOR OF 'THE LIFE AND DEATH OF JASON,'
'THE EARTHLY PARADISE,' &c.

LONDON:

ELLIS & WHITE, 29 NEW BOND STREET.

1882.

This is a crown 8vo. volume printed on laid paper,—217 pages with two preliminary leaves (half-title and title) and a leaf at the end bearing on both sides advertizements of Morris's works. The half-title reads "HOPES AND FEARS FOR ART" and has a blank verso. On the verso of the title, at the foot, is the imprint "LONDON/ PRINTED BY STRANGEWAYS & SONS,/ Tower Street, Upper St. Martin's Lane." This imprint is repeated in the centre of the verso of page 217. The paging is at the outer top corners as usual; and the head-lines give the titles of the several lectures, both recto and verso, in Italics. The cover is of "Morris green" cloth, unblocked, bearing a printed back-label with the legend "MORRIS'S/ LECTURES/ ON/ ART./ 4s. 6d." The edition consisted of 1000 copies; and the book was out by February 1882. Twenty-five copies were printed without variation on Whatman's hand-made paper, of demy 8vo. size, done up in blue paper boards with cream-white backs (bands showing), and a back-label worded like that of the ordinary copies but with no mention of price.

In this collection *The Decorative Arts* is reprinted as *The Lesser Arts* and stands first; next comes *The Art of the People* (a reprint of the Birmingham Address 1879 with the Defoe motto transferred to its head); *The Beauty of Life*, which follows, is a reprint of *Labour and Pleasure versus Labour and Sorrow*; next comes *Making the Best of it*, a paper read before the Trades Guild of Learning and the Birmingham Society of

7—2

Artists; and the book ends with *The Prospects of Architecture in Civilization*, an address delivered at the London (63) Institution. A second edition of 1000 copies was issued a year after the first. There is nothing special to record about it.

A crown 8vo. volume published in the same year as *Hopes and Fears for Art* has two more lectures by Morris in it—

(64)

LECTURES ON ART

DELIVERED IN SUPPORT OF THE

SOCIETY FOR THE PROTECTION OF ANCIENT BUILDINGS

BY

REGINALD STUART POOLE

| PROF. W. B. RICHMOND | J. T. MICKLETHWAITE |
| E. J. POYNTER, R.A. | WILLIAM MORRIS |

London

MACMILLAN AND CO.

1882

Morris wrote not far short of half the book, 106 pages out of 232 of the text, which text is preceded by the half-title LECTURES ON ART, with the publishers' monogram on the verso, the title-page with imprint at the foot of the verso, "*Printed by* R. & R. CLARK, *Edinburgh.*"—a preface of three pages by Mr. Micklethwaite, ending on page vii, the verso of which is blank, and two pages of "Contents." The pages are numbered in the outer corners; and there are head-lines giving the subjects of the several lectures in even capitals with the names of the authors in extremely small capitals in the inner corners. Morris's two lectures are *The History of Pattern Designing* and *The Lesser Arts of Life*.

Like most of Clark's work, the sheets are excellently printed in very black ink on very white paper. They are bound in a good green cloth into an entirely pleasant volume, with a plain ruled border round the sides ("blind") and the title lettered on the back in gold thus—"LECTURES/ ON/ ART/

Poole/ Richmond/ Poynter/ Micklethwaite/ Morris/ MACMILLAN & Co." The end-papers are white.

In 1882 Morris also wrote for the " Anti-scrape " a circular on Italian restorations,—to be distributed in Italy : it was translated into Italian (by a member of the Society), and was printed in that language,—two quarto pages of print and a blank leaf (half a sheet, post quarto). Page 1 is headed—

(65)

Società per la Protezione dei Monumenti Antichi.

At the head of the secretarial signatures is that of Morris.

There is one more pamphlet to describe before passing to those of the Socialist period. Its title is—

(66)

International Health Exhibition.
LONDON, 1884.

TEXTILE FABRICS.

A LECTURE

DELIVERED IN THE

LECTURE ROOM OF THE EXHIBITION,

JULY 11*th*, 1884.

BY

WILLIAM MORRIS.

PRINTED AND PUBLISHED FOR THE

Executive Council of the International Health Exhibition,
and for the Council of the Society of Arts,

BY

WILLIAM CLOWES AND SONS, Limited,
INTERNATIONAL HEALTH EXHIBITION
AND 13, CHARING CROSS, S.W.
1884.

This is an 8vo. of two sheets, one placed within the other and sewn through the fold, with a wrapper pasted on and the edges trimmed. On the verso of the title is the central imprint " LONDON :/ PRINTED BY WILLIAM CLOWES AND SONS, LIMITED,/ STAMFORD STREET AND CHARING CROSS." Page 3 contains the chairman's introduction of the lecturer to his audience. The lecture begins on page 4 and ends on page 29. Page 30 is blank. In the centre of page 31 the imprint is repeated ; and page 32 is blank. Pages 4 to 29 are numbered in the outer corners as usual ; and the head-lines throughout are " *TEX-TILE FABRICS.*" The wrapper is printed in brown ink on greenish grey paper. The wording differs slightly from the title-page and has an ornamental border surmounted with a crown. Outside the border are the words " issued by authority " and " price sixpence." Pages 2, 3, and 4 of the wrapper contain lists of conferences, lectures, and official publications.

SOCIALISM

LECTURES—POEMS
ARTICLES—TREATISES—PREFACES
AND NEWSPAPERS.

A SUMMARY
OF THE PRINCIPLES
OF
SOCIALISM

WRITTEN FOR

THE DEMOCRATIC FEDERATION,

BY

H. M. HYNDMAN & WILLIAM MORRIS.

THE WRAPPER OF "PRINCIPLES OF SOCIALISM" AS DESIGNED BY MORRIS, AND
PRINTED ON CREAM-TONED PAPER FOR THE FIRST EDITION.

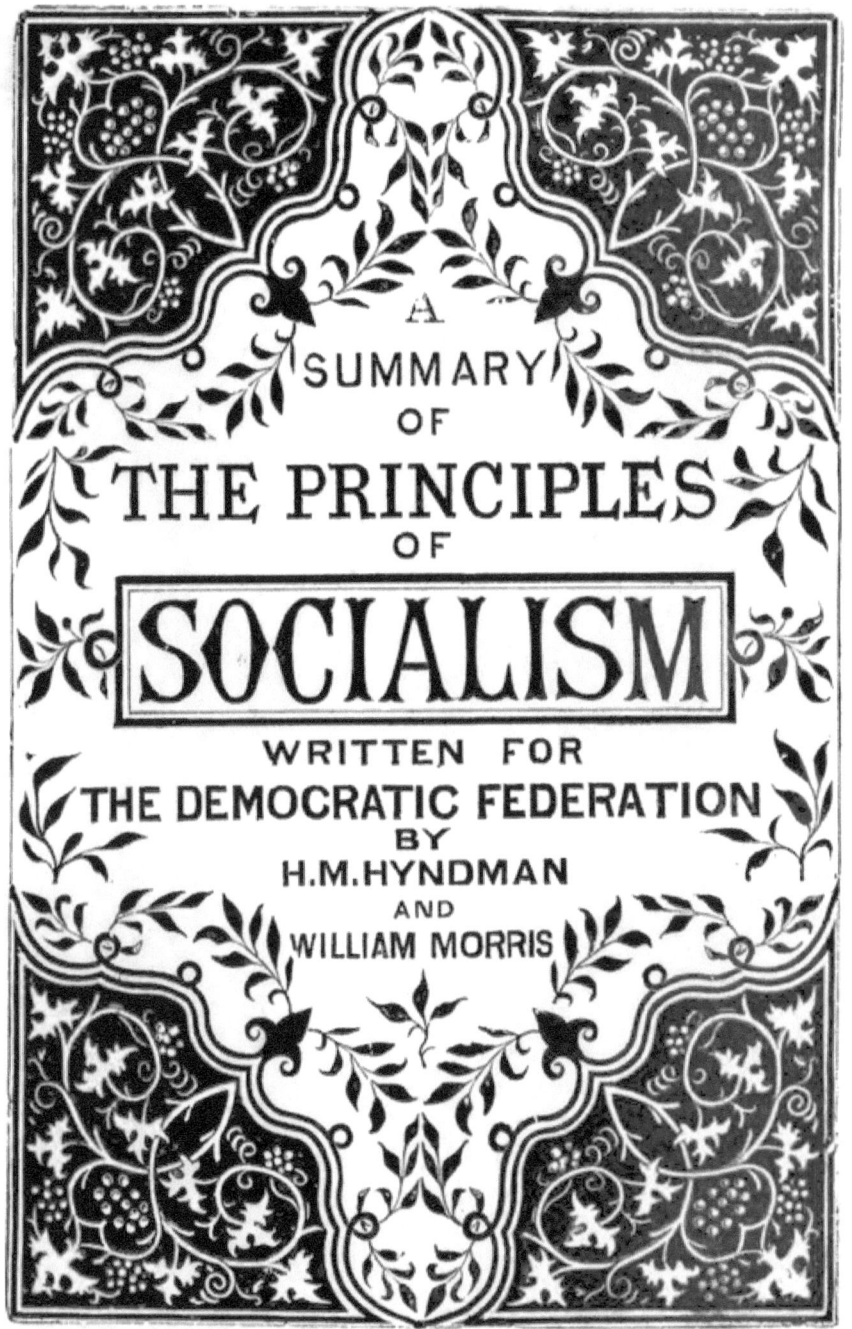

A
SUMMARY
OF
THE PRINCIPLES
OF
SOCIALISM
WRITTEN FOR
THE DEMOCRATIC FEDERATION
BY
H. M. HYNDMAN
AND
WILLIAM MORRIS

THE WRAPPER OF "PRINCIPLES OF SOCIALISM" AS RE-ARRANGED FOR THE
SECOND AND LATER ISSUES.

SOCIALISM:

Lectures — Poems — Articles — Treatises — Prefaces and Newspapers.

IT is a brusque transition from the Imperial crown on the wrapper of the lecture "published by authority" to the emblems which are to be found upon the long series of deliverances in support of socialism now to be chronicled. But the attentive reader of the lectures already mentioned would find no great reason for surprise at the direction which Morris's teaching soon took. Without discussing who it was that first turned the poet's thoughts towards socialism, we must note, in connexion with the year 1884, the foundation of Mr. H. M. Hyndman's paper, *Justice*, the organ of the Social-Democratic Federation. In that year Morris was a constant contributor; and he signed with others the address of the Federation to the Trades' Unions of Great Britain, dated September 1884 and published in No. 34. Half a dozen articles in the next fifteen numbers finished the tale of his contributions to *Justice* for the time being; for the historic split had come; and on the 30th of December 1884 the Provisional Council of the Socialist League signed the renowned Manifesto of that new sect of socialists. But before the split Morris had joined Mr. Hyndman in producing the pamphlet for the cover of which the beautiful design facing this page was drawn; and to this period belong a few other pamphlets, the titles of which shall be set out as briefly as possible with such details as are necessary. It will be noticed that the ill-starred "Modern Press" had the distinction of printing Morris's earliest socialist books or booklets both in prose and in verse, that is to say if the order here adopted is chronologically correct, a point upon which I am not quite certain. There is a strong family likeness between these pamphlets of what I

will call the pre-Crane era. When Mr. Walter Crane became
a socialist, in the circumstances which he has himself recounted in *Justice,* his great gifts as a designer were ever at the
service of the cause; and some of his socialist cartoons and
headings are as truly admirable as any of his black and white
work. Of the first pamphlet now to be described the title-page
is as follows :—

(67)

A

SUMMARY

OF THE

PRINCIPLES OF SOCIALISM

Written for the Democratic Federation,

BY

H. M. HYNDMAN AND WILLIAM MORRIS.

LONDON :
THE MODERN PRESS,
13 AND 14 PATERNOSTER ROW, E.C.
1884.

This is a crown 8vo. sewn and trimmed,—64 pages counting
the title and blank verso and one blank leaf at the end. The
pages are numbered centrally in arabic figures. Pages 2, 3
and 4 of the wrapper are blank. It is extremely
(68—69) rare. There is an issue of the same year on slightly
thinner paper, differing from the first in that it is
wire-stitched, with a pink wrapper of which the ornamentation
is rearranged as shown opposite, and the 2nd, 3rd and 4th
pages filled with advertizements, as is the last leaf (pp. 63
and 64). Mr. William Reeves, who now publishes the pamphlet, issues it with the pink rearranged wrapper, different
advertizements, and a title-page similarly worded, but with the
imprint "LONDON :/ WILLIAM REEVES, 185, FLEET
STREET, E.C./ 1896." This issue is stabbed through and
sewn with thread. All three have the wrappers stuck on
after the sheets are fastened together. Towards the close of
1884 Mr. Reeves published Mr. Sketchley's *Review of European
Society,* to which Morris contributed a brief introduction (two
pages of small type) dated *September 29th 1884.* It is a

trimmed post 8vo. of 240 pages all told, sewn and issued in a pale blue wrapper with white end papers. The title (repeated on the wrapper, without the quotation from Carlyle) is—

(70)

A REVIEW OF/ EUROPEAN SOCIETY,/ WITH AN/ EXPOSITION AND VINDICATION/ OF THE PRINCIPLES OF/ SOCIAL DEMOCRACY./ BY J. SKETCHLEY,/ Author of "Popery, its Supporters and Opponents," "The Irish/ Question," "The Funding System," "German Democracy," &c./ [quotation from Carlyle] *PRICE EIGHTEENPENCE./* LONDON :/ W. REEVES, 185, FLEET STREET, E.C./ BIRMINGHAM :/ J. SKETCHLEY, 348, CHEAPSIDE./ [ALL RIGHTS RESERVED.]

Of this the first edition is still in stock, but with a fresh wrapper printed in dark blue ink (the first is in black) on pale blue paper, and with the imprint "LONDON :/ WILLIAM REEVES, 185, FLEET STREET, E.C."

Morris was now writing and printing in the Socialist periodical press the series of poems known as *Chants for Socialists.* One of the rarest of Socialist items is the "Modern Press" issue of *The Day is Coming.* The title is—

(71)

DEMOCRATIC FEDERATION.

———◆———

C H A N T S   F O R   S O C I A L I S T S :

No. I.

T H E   D A Y   I S   C O M I N G.

BY

WILLIAM MORRIS,

Author of " The Earthly Paradise," etc.

————

LONDON :
REEVES, 185, FLEET STREET, E.C.

It is a trimmed crown 8vo. of eight pages including the title and blank verso. The head-lines (pages 4 to 8) are, verso,

"*CHANTS FOR SOCIALISTS*," recto, "*THE DAY IS COMING*." The imprint at foot of page 8 is, below a thin rule, " Printed at The Modern Press, 13 & 14, Paternoster Row, London." There is a wrapper of very pale buff paper, repeating the title with the addition of " Price One Penny " after " Earthly Paradise, etc." Page 2 of it is blank : pages 3 and 4 bear advertizements. Equally interesting and rare is the pamphlet of which the following is the title :—

(72)

THE VOICE OF TOIL:

ALL FOR THE CAUSE.

TWO CHANTS

FOR

SOCIALISTS.

BY

WILLIAM MORRIS.

———

LONDON :
REPRINTED FROM "JUSTICE,"
The Organ of the Social Democratic Federation.
(*Price One Penny.*)

This is an untrimmed crown 8vo. The eight pages are filled by the two poems ; and the title only occurs on a pale primrose-coloured wrapper of which pages 2, 3, and 4 are blank. The pages are numbered centrally in arabic figures ; and at the foot of page 8 is the imprint, below a thin rule, " PRINTED AT THE OFFICE OF ' JUSTICE.' " The next pamphlet raises the blood-red banner of socialism by means of its wrapper, though the subject is only indirectly socialistic :—

(73)

THE GOD OF THE POOR.

BY

WILLIAM MORRIS,
AUTHOR OF "THE EARTHLY PARADISE."

———

ORIGINALLY PUBLISHED IN THE
"FORTNIGHTLY REVIEW," AUGUST 1, 1868.

This again is an untrimmed crown 8vo. of eight pages, but this time with a regular title-page and six pages of text, numbered centrally in arabic figures. It is sewn into a red wrapper on which the upper part of the title is reproduced, with the imprint " LONDON :/ Printed at the Office of "Justice,"/ *The Organ of the Social Democratic Federation./ (Price One Penny.)*." Pages 2, 3 and 4 of the wrapper are blank. The refrain *Deus est Deus pauperum*, instead of following each of the 52 stanzas as in *The Fortnightly Review*, is only printed after the first and last.

There is one more booklet belonging to 1884 :

(74)

Art and Socialism : a Lecture delivered [January 23rd, 1884] before the Secular Society of *Leicester*, by WILLIAM MORRIS, author of " *The Earthly Paradise*," etc.

And *Watchman : What of the Night ?*

Cum Privilegio Auctoris.

Imprinted for E. E. M. and W. L. S. Anno 1884.

Sold by W. REEVES, 185, Fleet St., London, E.C.; and by HEYWOODS, London and Manchester.

How long after the delivery of the lecture this was printed I know not. The title is a little differently worded upon the wrapper, printed in red on a salmon-coloured ground, and has " PRICE 3D." at foot. The booklet is a crown 16mo. of 3¾ sheets, placed one within another and sewn into the wrapper through one fold. The first page bears the Leek book-mark and the words " Reprint Number VII./ *Art and Socialism :/ a Statement of the Aims and Ideals/ of the English Socialists of To-day*." On the versos of this and the title are quotations from Ruskin and Wordsworth. The Lecture fills pages 5 to 58.

Then—after a fresh half-title, "*Watchman: What of the Night?*"—come extracts from Swinburne, Meredith, Carlyle, Whitman, Blake, et al., and a lot of advertizements, completing 88 pages in all. There are large-paper copies (Dutch handmade) of which the wrappers are printed in red ink on primrose-coloured paper. Of these special copies the price was 1s.

THE COMMONWEAL

The Official Journal of the Socialist League.

Early in 1885 *The Commonweal* was started as the monthly organ of The Socialist League. Eleven numbers, dated February to December, were published in the year. In the first the Manifesto appeared, as did also a new "Chant for Socialists," *The March of the Workers.* The second number contained *The Message of the March Wind* (also a "Chant for Socialists"); but in the third (April) number it was announced that Morris would follow the fortunes of the lovers in *The Message*, under the title of *The Pilgrims of Hope*, the second section of which accordingly appeared. The first number is bare of decoration,—just plain homely type throughout. The word "Commonweal" in the heading was set in good "old-faced" capitals an inch high, with the word "the" above it in ugly block letters. In the second number the "the" was done to match the "Commonweal," and Morris had designed a tracery of willow for a background to this heading, which remained in use till the end. By April Mr. Crane's two admirable headings were ready; and they appeared in No. 3. The "Freedom, Equality, and Fraternity" design appeared in the centre of the paper, at the head of the general notices, and was also retained till the end. The Socialist League design was placed on the last page at the head of a report about the League. In No. 4, No. 5, and No. 6 it reappeared as a heading for League reports; but after that it was reserved for the pamphlets, save that a reduction from it was occasionally inserted in the advertizement columns.

HEADINGS DESIGNED BY WALTER CRANE.

8

The first independent issue of the Manifesto was a half-sheet crown 8vo. pamphlet without title-page or wrapper, headed "PRICE ONE PENNY.]/ THE/ MANIFESTO/ OF/ THE (75) SOCIALIST LEAGUE." This was issued before the end of January 1885 ; and an advertizement on the 8th page announces the first number of *The Common-weal* for "January 28th." At the foot of the page is the imprint, below a thin rule, "Printed by ARTHUR BONNER, 63, Fleet Street, London, E.C.—1885." After Mr. Crane's League design had been done, a white wrapper was added forming the following title:—

THE MANIFESTO

OF

WRITTEN BY WILLIAM MORRIS,

SIGNED BY THE PROVISIONAL COUNCIL AT THE FOUNDATION OF THE LEAGUE ON 30TH DEC. 1884, AND ADOPTED AT

THE GENERAL CONFERENCE

Held at FARRINGDON HALL, LONDON, on July 5th, 1885.

LONDON:
Socialist League Office,
13, FARRINGDON ROAD, HOLBORN VIADUCT, E.C.

—

1885.

An enlarged Manifesto pamphlet was issued the same year, —a crown 8vo. sheet. On the verso of the title-page is a note signed by E. Belfort Bax and William Morris. The Manifesto ends on page 8,—the notes, of which this is the first edition, on page 14. On page 15 is a list of "Socialist League Lecturers," and on page 16 advertizements of League literature. Though generally circulated without a wrapper, there are copies—but these are rare—in a Turner-grey wrapper on which the title is repeated with an additional line below the design, "WRITTEN BY WILLIAM MORRIS," and the words "price one penny" omitted. The title-page is as follows:—

8—2

(76)

THE MANIFESTO

OF

SIGNED BY THE PROVISIONAL COUNCIL AT THE FOUNDATION OF THE
LEAGUE ON 30TH DEC. 1884, AND ADOPTED AT

THE GENERAL CONFERENCE

Held at FARRINGDON HALL, LONDON, on JULY 5th, 1885.

——o——

A New Edition, Annotated by
WILLIAM MORRIS AND E. BELFORT BAX.

LONDON :
Socialist League Office,
13 FARRINGDON ROAD, HOLBORN VIADUCT, E.C.
1885.
PRICE ONE PENNY.

The League gave an entertainment in June, for which Morris
wrote a prologue. It appeared in *The Commonweal* and also
exists as a pamphlet with the following title :—

(77)

SOCIALISTS AT PLAY.

BY
WILLIAM MORRIS.

*Prologue
Spoken at the Entertainment of
the Socialist League :*

*SOUTH PLACE INSTITUTE,
June 11,*
1885.

It is a royal 16mo. of 8 pages (a quarter of a sheet), with half-title, "SOCIALISTS AT PLAY," title with blank verso, and 4 pages of text, sewn into a blood-red wrapper on which the title is repeated, and of which pages 2, 3 and 4 are blank. It was not very long after the entertainment at the South Place Institute that the Socialist League adopted with due solemnity and promulgated with due formality a constitution and a brief code of rules. These were embodied in a pamphlet of which the title is as follows :—

(78)

CONSTITUTION AND RULES
ADOPTED AT
THE GENERAL CONFERENCE

Held at FARRINGDON HALL, LONDON, on JULY 5th,
1885.

LONDON :
Socialist League Office,
13 FARRINGDON ROAD, HOLBORN VIADUCT, E.C.

—

1885.

This publication consists of a crown 8vo. half-sheet, trimmed and stitched into a green wrapper. The Constitution and Rules fill the eight pages, which are numbered centrally ; and there is no title-page save that on the wrapper, of which page 2 is blank, while pages 3 and 4 have the list of Lecturers and the advertizements. Next comes the first edition of the *Chants for Socialists* as a whole. This is not the crown 8vo. sheet frequently offered by the booksellers as the first edition, but an uncut demy 8vo., very roughly printed, though with a sightly title-page, as follows :—

(79)

CHANTS FOR SOCIALISTS

BY

WILLIAM MORRIS.

Contents :

1. THE DAY IS COMING.
2. THE VOICE OF TOIL.
3. ALL FOR THE CAUSE.
4. NO MASTER.
5. THE MARCH OF THE WORKERS.
6. THE MESSAGE OF THE MARCH WIND.

PRICE ONE PENNY.

PUBLISHED AT

THE SOCIALIST LEAGUE OFFICE, 27 FARRINGDON STREET,
LONDON, E.C.

1885.

It was first issued unsewn, merely folded. On the verso of the title is an extract from a lecture by Morris. There are no head-lines ; but the pages are numbered in the outer corners. Page 16 has Mr. Crane's *Commonweal* block at the top, with advertizements of the paper &c., and at foot, beneath a thin rule, the imprint " Printed and published by W. Morris and J. Lane at 27 Farringdon St., London, E.C." Copies are occasionally found in a red wrapper with the legend " CHANTS/ FOR/ SOCIALISTS/ BY/ William Morris./ 1885." But they were not originally issued in wrappers.

A second edition of the *Chants for Socialists* was printed the same year: it was done in crown 8vo. in order to make up or bind with *The Socialist Platform,* which is of that size; and the "chant" *Down among the Dead Men* was added. The title of this single sheet (16 pages) is—

(80)

THE SOCIALIST LEAGUE

CHANTS FOR SOCIALISTS

BY

WILLIAM MORRIS.

CONTENTS:

The Day is Coming.
The Voice of Toil.
The Message of the March Wind

No Master.
All for the Cause.
The March of the Workers.

Down Among the Dead Men.

LONDON :

Socialist League Office,

13 FARRINGDON ROAD, HOLBORN VIADUCT, E.C.

1885.

PRICE ONE PENNY.

There are head-lines to this edition—versos "CHANTS FOR SOCIALISTS"—rectos, the names of the individual chants; and the paging is in the outer corners. There is no imprint at the end. Collectors of first editions should beware of this issue, of which copies are constantly catalogued as of (81) the first edition. Another crown 8vo. edition was printed in 1892, similar to that of 1885, but with the address "40, Berner Street, Commercial Road, E." Of *The Socialist Platform,* No. 1 and No. 2 have the following titles :—

(82—83)

THE SOCIALIST PLATFORM.—No. 1.

ADDRESS TO
TRADES' UNIONS.

ISSUED BY THE

Council of the Socialist League.

PRICE ONE PENNY.

LONDON:
SOCIALIST LEAGUE OFFICE,
27 FARRINGDON STREET, E.C.

1885.

THE SOCIALIST PLATFORM.—No. 2.

USEFUL WORK
V.
USELESS TOIL

BY

WILLIAM MORRIS.

PRICE ONE PENNY.

LONDON:
SOCIALIST LEAGUE OFFICE,
13 FARRINGDON ROAD, HOLBORN VIADUCT, E.C.

1885.

Of No. 1 the preface only is signed by Morris with Mr. Bax, as joint editors. The address is stated in the heading to be written by Mr. Bax. Pages 13 to 15 are an Appendix by Mr. Joseph Lane ; and page 16 has Mr. Crane's *Commonweal* block at the head of advertizements. No. 2, on the other hand, is a genuine *editio princeps*, of which the contents had been delivered in lecture form and printed in *Justice*. It is trimmed and sewn, 24 pages, with a preface by the editors on the verso of the title, 21 pages of text ending on page 39, and on page 40 the *Commonweal* block at the head of advertize-ments. At the foot, below a thin rule, is the imprint "Printed and published by WILLIAM MORRIS and JOSEPH LANE, at 13 Farringdon Rd. London." In 1893 this pamphlet was reprinted apart from the *Platform* by the Hammer-
(84) smith Socialist Society with their imprint and Mr. Crane's Labour and Justice design. It is a twenty-page penny pamphlet. In the next number Morris is only in-directly concerned : the title is—" *The Socialist Platform.—No. 3./* [League block]/ *The Factory Hell./ by/ Edward Aveling & Eleanor Marx Aveling./ Price One Penny./*
(85) *London :/ Socialist League Office,/* 13 *Farringdon Road, Holborn Viaduct, E.C./ 1885."* This is one sheet. The text begins on the verso of the title, and carries the paging on to page 56, which ends with the same imprint as No. 2.

Beside *The Commonweal* and the *Platform*, there were numerous sheets and leaflets produced at this time. Morris wrote a crown 8vo. half-sheet, without wrapper or title-page, signed and dated at the end "THE COUNCIL OF THE SOCIALIST LEAGUE—*November, 1885."* It is headed

(86)

PRICE ONE HALFPENNY.

FOR WHOM SHALL WE VOTE ?

ADDRESSED TO THE WORKING-MEN ELECTORS OF GREAT BRITAIN.

At the end, below a thin rule, is the imprint " Printed and Published at the ' Commonweal ' Office, 13 Farringdon Road, London, E.C." He also wrote an address which was printed on both sides of a single 8vo. leaf headed—

No. 11.]

WHAT SOCIALISTS WANT.

At the end, below a thin rule, is the imprint "*Issued by the Hammersmith Branch of the Socialist League, Kelmscott| House, Upper Mall, Hammersmith, W.   Lectures and discussion every|*

Sunday evening at 8 o'clock. Open free to. all."   The Branch was conducted, as might be supposed, not without regard to the adornments of life.   The card of membership, a folding card measuring 6 inches by 4½, bears a charming design by Mr. Crane; and those who have their cards still may please themselves with the thought that they possess, with the poet's autograph, if not a positive portrait of him in the punning character of a smith hammering, at least a stalwart man with a handsome face intentionally of the Morris type.

The year 1886 was very productive. *The Commonweal,* a monthly journal in 1885, appeared weekly after the April number of 1886 ; and Morris contributed to that year's volume not only the complement of *The Pilgrims of Hope,* a considerable part of *Socialism from the Root Up* (with Mr. Bax), *An Old Story Retold* (*A King's Lesson*), and a great part of *A Dream of John Ball,* but also a large number of articles and " Notes on Passing Events." In Edinburgh one of his Socialist lectures was printed with the following title :—

(88)

CLAIMS OF LABOUR LECTURES—No. 5.

THE LABOUR QUESTION

FROM THE

SOCIALIST STANDPOINT.

BY WILLIAM MORRIS.

EDINBURGH
CO-OPERATIVE PRINTING COMPANY LIMITED,
BRISTO PLACE.
1886.

PRICE ONE PENNY.

This appears to be a single sheet of double crown paper. It is well printed, but trimmed and metal-fastened, with one fastener through the centre. On the verso of the title is a note relating to the series. The Lecture begins on page 3 with a dropped head. Pages 4 to 29 are numbered centrally in Arabic figures ; 30 and 31 are blank ; 32 is a page of advertizements (89) about Claims of Labour Lectures &c. The whole series including this of Morris's was reprinted as a crown 8vo. volume done up in cloth and sold at a popular price. The next pamphlet brings us back to London :—

(90)

THE SOCIALIST PLATFORM.—No. 4.

A SHORT ACCOUNT
OF THE
COMMUNE OF PARIS.

BY

E. BELFORT BAX, VICTOR DAVE

AND

WILLIAM MORRIS.

PRICE TWOPENCE.

LONDON:
SOCIALIST LEAGUE OFFICE,
13, FARRINGDON ROAD, HOLBORN VIADUCT, E.C.
1886.

On the verso of the title this crown 8vo. pamphlet has a quotation from Meredith's *Poems and Lyrics of the Joy of Earth.* Opposite this the short account starts with a dropped head. Pages 60 to 79 (for the paging is continuous from No. 3) are numbered in the outer corners. The head-lines are, versos "*The Socialist Platform,*" rectos "The Paris Commune." Page 80 contains Socialist advertizements. The 5th No. has nothing of Morris's in it, and needs only to be described here as part of a whole in which he is the chief writer. The (91) title is—"*The Socialist Platform.—No. 5.|* [League block]*| Organized Labour.| The Duty of the Trades' Unions| In relation to Socialism.| By| Thomas Binning| (London Society of Compositors).| Price one Penny.| London:| Socialist League Office,| 13 Farringdon Road, Holborn Viaduct, E.C.| 1886.*" A Lecture delivered by Morris at Norwich, printed in *Daylight,* was reprinted in 8 columns on both sides of an unfolded single sheet, headed as follows :—

(92)

SOCIALISM.

A LECTURE delivered under the auspices of the Norwich
Branch of the Socialist League, at/ the Victoria Hall, Norwich,
on Monday evening, March 8th, 1886, by/

MR. WILLIAM MORRIS.

Reprinted from " Daylight."

There is no imprint. The sub-title is in two lines. By the
beginning of July the end of *The Pilgrims of Hope* had appeared
in *The Commonweal.* I could not persuade its author to
reprint it: he considered it wanted more revision than he
could give it at the time. I threatened to reprint it in a decent
way myself, privately of course ; and, as he did not forbid me,
I did so. The booklet, intended to be uniform with his " square
crown 8vo." volumes of long-line poems, consists of a half-title,
" THE/ PILGRIMS OF HOPE," a title, a list of contents, a
two-page prefatory note, a second half-title, pages 9 to 69 of
text, a blank leaf, and a grey wrapper. The title-page reads
as follows :—

(93)

THE

PILGRIMS OF HOPE

A POEM

IN THIRTEEN BOOKS

BY

WILLIAM MORRIS

LONDON :

BROUGHT TOGETHER FROM "THE COMMONWEAL"

For March, April, May, June, August, September, & November, 1885,
And January, March, April, May 8, June 5, & July 3,

MDCCCLXXXVI.

The first page of the wrapper bears the title " THE/
PILGRIMS OF HOPE/ BY/ WILLIAM MORRIS." All
unspecified versos are blank. I grieve to say the edges are
trimmed,—contrary to express orders. Otherwise the print is

not one to be ashamed of, but rather choice. It and the next, published by Morris himself, compare very favourably with the League prints. The next is a pretty little 40-page demy 16mo. in a Turner-grey wrapper, which was on sale by the middle of February 1887. The title is—

(94)

THE AIMS OF ART

BY

WILLIAM MORRIS

AUTHOR OF "THE EARTHLY PARADISE" ETC

LONDON

OFFICE OF "THE COMMONWEAL"

13 FARRINGDON ROAD

1887

This is repeated on the wrapper. Page 3 of the book has a dropped head; pages 4 to 39 are numbered in the outer corners and have the head-line "*THE AIMS OF ART*"; and at foot of page 39 is the imprint, below a thin rule, "LONDON :/ STRANGEWAYS AND SONS, Tower Street, St. Martin's Lane, W.C." All unspecified pages are blank. There are copies on Whatman's hand-made paper, with hand-made wrappers. Before the close of the spring came out one half of the translation of Homer's Odyssey: the title-pages of this book are—

(95)

THE

ODYSSEY OF HOMER

DONE INTO ENGLISH VERSE

BY

WILLIAM MORRIS,

AUTHOR OF THE EARTHLY PARADISE.

IN TWO VOLUMES.

VOL. I. [II.]

LONDON:

REEVES & TURNER, 196 STRAND.

MDCCCLXXXVII.

Although printed in eights, this book may be most nearly described as a foolscap quarto. Each volume consists of twelve books of the Odyssey, preceded by four leaves—namely the half-title reading "THE ODYSSEY OF HOMER," title, and 3-page "Contents." The verso pages ii, iv, and viii are blank in both volumes. In Volume I. the text consists of 230 pages, and is followed by a blank leaf: in Volume II. the text is 218 pages, and ends on page 450, the paging of the two volumes being continuous. At the foot of page 450, below a thin rule, is the imprint "LONDON/ Printed by STRANGEWAYS & SONS, Tower Street, Cambridge Circus." The book is put up in blue paper boards with white rounded backs and printed labels of which the legend is "THE/ ODYSSEY/ OF/ HOMER./ W. MORRIS./ VOL. I. [II.]/ *Price 12s.*" The price was that of each volume; for the ordinary copies of this first edition are on hand-made paper—Dutch, I think; but there are no water-marks. The book is quite untrimmed, and is of a most agreeable appearance,—handsome enough for anything. Nevertheless there were large-paper copies printed on Dickenson's hand-made paper, of crown quarto size, bound in mottled paper boards of a dark olive colour with more or less yellow in flecks, and backed with vellum. The labels read as in the ordinary copies but that no price is given on them. Vol. I., of both sizes, came out in April 1887,—Vol. II. in November.

It will not be supposed that these two beautiful volumes were paged continuously without a practical reason. The object, of course, was to avoid alterations for the ultimate popular edition; for an edition on hand-made paper published at the price of 24s. was not likely to be a large edition. It was soon consumed, and the book was then issued on ordinary machine-made paper in one volume, uniform with *Sigurd the Volsung* and the translation of *The Æneid.* The (96—97) *Odyssey* is now included in Messrs. Longman's ten-volume edition of the poetical works, with a label reading "THE /POETICAL/ WORKS OF/ WILLIAM/ MORRIS./ THE/ ODYSSEY/ OF/ HOMER./ *Six Shillings.*"

Late in the same year appeared the crown 8vo. blue-wrappered play familiarly known as "Nupkins," rather better printed than most of the League prints. The title is—

(98)

THE

TABLES TURNED;

OR,

NUPKINS AWAKENED

A Socialist Interlude

BY

WILLIAM MORRIS

AUTHOR OF 'THE EARTHLY PARADISE.'

*As for the first time played at the Hall of the Socialist League
on Saturday October 15, 1887*

LONDON:

OFFICE OF "THE COMMONWEAL"

13 FARRINGDON ROAD, E.C.

1887

All Rights Reserved

This title is on the wrapper (there is no other title-page): on
the verso appear the names of the dramatis personæ and the
original cast, from which we learn that Morris supported the
character of the Archbishop of Canterbury, and his daughter
May (now Mrs. Sparling) that of Mary Pinch. The play is
apparently on a single sheet of double crown paper. It is
stitched into its wrapper and trimmed. The paging is as
usual; and the head-lines, versos "*The Tables Turned; or,*"
rectos "*Nupkins Awakened.*" The last page has the double
title as head-line, and, at its foot, the imprint "Printed and
Published at the COMMONWEAL Office, 13 Farringdon Road,
London, E.C." Pages 3 and 4 of the wrapper are filled by
advertizements.

The death of Alfred Linnell in the Trafalgar Square dis-
turbances of November 1887 called forth from Morris a beautiful dirge, and from Mr. Crane a design in which the artist
triumphs over the obvious difficulties of making a mounted
policeman decorative. A pamphlet consisting of a half-sheet,
royal 8vo., was printed and sold in the streets with the title of
which a reduced copy is given opposite. All the 8 pages have
mourning borders. The title is page 1; pages 2 to 4 contain

for H Buxton Forman William Morris

SOLD FOR THE BENEFIT OF LINNELL'S ORPHANS.

ALFRED LINNELL

Killed in Trafalgar Square,

NOVEMBER 20, 1887.

A DEATH SONG,

BY MR. W. MORRIS.

Memorial Design by Mr. Walter Crane.

PRICE ONE PENNY.

REDUCED FAC-SIMILE OF TITLE-PAGE.

9

an account of Linnell's death ; on pages 5 to 7 and the top of 8 the words appear set to music by Mr. Malcolm Lawson ; and the dirge is printed on the lower part of page 8, at foot of which is the imprint "Printed and Published by RICHARD LAMBERT, at 2, Northumberland-street, Strand, in the Parish of St. Martin's-in-the-Fields." The dropped head of page 2 and all verso head-lines read *"ALFRED LINNELL."* The recto head-lines are (page 3) *" KILLED IN TRAFALGAR SQUARE,"* and (pages 5 and 6) *" A DEATH SONG."*

On the 5th of December Morris finished a Preface of four pages to the crown 8vo. treatise of which the title is—

(100)

THE/ PRINCIPLES OF SOCIALISM/ MADE PLAIN ;/ AND/ OBJECTIONS, METHODS, AND QUACK RE-MEDIES/ FOR POVERTY CONSIDERED./ BY/ FRANK FAIRMAN./ WITH/ PREFACE BY WILLIAM MORRIS/ London :/ WILLIAM REEVES, 185, FLEET STREET, E.C./ 1888.

The book has viii + 148 pages, 4 more of advertizements, and a printed wrapper differing at page 1 from the title-page. On page 4 of it, *Justice, The Commonweal*, &c. are advertized. The original wrapper was primrose-coloured : the same edition is still on sale, but with a pale blue wrapper. The following passage from the preface shows how thoughtfully Morris examined the book before god-fathering it :

" It seems to me that the constitutional or parliamentary method which he advocates would involve loss of energy, disappointment, and discouragement ; that it would bear with it the almost inevitable danger of the people's eyes being directed to the immediate struggle, losing sight of the ultimate aim ; of their being befooled by those very concessions which the author speaks of as likely to be offered so eagerly by the present political parties ; and, judging by the signs of the times, I cannot help thinking that the necessities of the miserable, ever increasing as the old system gets closer to its inevitable ruin, will outrun the slow process of converting parliament from a mere committee of the landlords and capitalists into a popular body representing the best aspirations of the workers. Moreover socialists, unless they abandon their principles, cannot

9—2

help showing their hand from the first, and consequently even moderate measures will always be looked on with suspicion coming from them, and concessions which would have been granted without much resistance to the Radicals twenty or even ten years ago, if they had been demanded, will be sternly refused to the Socialist demand. In the days in which I am now writing, there are not lacking signs that the reactionists, driven by the fear of the advancing wave of revolution, are making up their minds to make a stand on the ground of mere brute force, which at present they are able to command."

The next Socialist pamphlet on our list was printed about the 24th of July 1888 :—

(101)

"The Socialist Platform."—No. 6.

TRUE AND FALSE
SOCIETY

BY

WILLIAM MORRIS

PRICE ONE PENNY

LONDON:
SOCIALIST LEAGUE OFFICE
13 FARRINGDON ROAD, E.C.
1888

The verso of the title is blank. Page 3 has a dropped head. Pages 4 to 22 (the text) have verso head-lines " *The Socialist Platform*" and recto head-lines " *True and False Society.*" Page 23 is blank. Page 24 is filled with advertizements headed " Socialist Literature." The Scheme of doing up the *Platform* with *Chants for Socialists* (second edition) was more than realized by means of the crown 8vo. volume of which the title is—

(102)

THE SOCIALIST PLATFORM

WRITTEN BY SEVERAL HANDS FOR

TOGETHER WITH

THE MANIFESTO

AND

CHANTS FOR SOCIALISTS

BY

WILLIAM MORRIS.

LONDON :
Socialist League Office
13, FARRINGDON ROAD, HOLBORN VIADUCT, E.C
1888.

Price One Shilling.

This title, with a blank verso, is followed by a " Contents," also
with blank verso.   The " Contents " is a list of the pamphlets
and their authors.   The book is simply composed of the Manifesto with Notes, the six numbers of the *Platform*, and the
Chants,—the actual pamphlets, apparently.   The special title
and " Contents " are repeated on the first and last pages of a
green wrapper, nearly the same colour as that of the *Constitution and Rules.*   Of *True and False Society*, as of
(103)   *Useful Work v. Useless Toil*, there is a twenty-page
penny issue dated 1893, with the imprint of the
Hammersmith Socialist Society, and with the Labour and
Justice design which Mr. Crane did for the Society. (See
page 113.)

SIGNS OF CHANGE

JOHN BALL—THE HOUSE OF THE WOLFINGS
THE ROOTS OF THE MOUNTAINS
NEWS FROM NOWHERE

PORTRAIT BOOK-PLATE DESIGNED BY WALTER CRANE FOR THE HAMMER-
SMITH BRANCH OF THE SOCIALIST LEAGUE TO INSERT IN A SET OF
BOOKS PRESENTED TO MORRIS'S DAUGHTER MAY ON HER MARRIAGE TO
H. HALLIDAY SPARLING.

SIGNS OF CHANGE:

John Ball—The House of the Wolfings—The Roots of the Mountains—News from Nowhere.

WHILE 1888 was still young, Morris completed the preparation of a volume of his lectures, issued early in May under the title—

(104)

SIGNS OF CHANGE
Seven Lectures
DELIVERED ON VARIOUS OCCASIONS

By
WILLIAM MORRIS
AUTHOR OF
"THE EARTHLY PARADISE"

LONDON
REEVES AND TURNER
196 STRAND
1888

In this crown 8vo. volume of xii + 204 pages including advertizements at beginning and end, *The Aims of Art* and *Useful Work* are reprinted, with (1) *How we Live and How we Might Live*, (2) *Whigs, Democrats, and Socialists*, and (3) *Feudal England*, from *The Commonweal*, and *The Hopes of Civilization* and *Dawn of a New Epoch* from the manuscripts. The ordinary copies are in dark red cloth lettered on the back, " SIGNS/ OF/ CHANGE/ W. MORRIS/ REEVES & TURNER." There are large-paper (hand-made) copies, demy 8vo., done up in cream-coloured buckram, with a back-label reading " SIGNS/ OF/

CHANGE/ Seven Lectures/ BY/ W. MORRIS/ Large Paper."
The book was printed in London at the Ballantyne Press : the
large copies are handsome.

There were not wanting " signs of change " in the attitude
of Morris's mind. The artist in him was getting the upper
hand again. Almost all he did, to the end, had something in
it for " the cause"; and I believe he would have held to
socialist principles to the end if his life had been prolonged
another quarter of a century. But *militant* socialism had
shown him its seamy side ; and, though *post hoc* may not be
propter hoc, it seems to me that, as the literary artist became
more and more thoroughly reawakened, the differences between
him and the more pronounced of the militant sect tended more
and more towards the ultimate breach. In *John Ball* he must
have experienced keen creative joy ; but that admirable book
is but the beginning of the great things which the literary artist
had in store for us so soon as the militant socialist should give
him leave.

Although *John Ball* had been finished in *The Commonweal*
by the 22nd of January 1887, it was not republished as a book
till April 1888, when it came out with the title—

(105)

A DREAM OF JOHN BALL

AND

A KING'S LESSON.

(REPRINTED FROM THE 'COMMONWEAL.')

BY

WILLIAM MORRIS,

AUTHOR OF
'THE EARTHLY PARADISE,' ETC.

With an Illustration by EDWARD BURNE-JONES.

LONDON :
REEVES & TURNER, 196 STRAND.
MDCCCLXXXVIII.

Though worked in eights, this is a royal 16mo. It has a blank-verso'd half-title, "A DREAM OF JOHN BALL/ AND/ A KING'S LESSON." preceded by a blank leaf. The title is followed by the " Contents " (pages vii and viii), after which is inserted Sir Edward Burne-Jones's etching of the subject described in the couplet

> When Adam delved and Eve span
> Who was then the gentleman ?

The story occupies 143 pages. At the foot of the last, below a thin rule, is the imprint " LONDON/ Printed by STRANGEWAYS & SONS, Tower Street, Cambridge Circus, W.C." Page 144 is blank, and is followed by an inserted leaf of advertizements about Morris's works. The binding is of dark red cloth, un-blocked, with a paper label reading " A/ DREAM/ OF/ JOHN/ BALL/ &c./ BY/ W. MORRIS/ 4s. 6d." The price is cut off the label for the large-paper copies, which are on Dickens's hand-made paper, pot quarto, half-bound in vellum with marble-paper sides. When the book was reprinted at the Kelmscott Press, the frontispiece was reproduced as a wood-cut with a border of the author's designing. Though the size of a crown 8vo., the Kelmscott edition is, literally, a quarto, with a deckel edge all round every sheet of 8 pages (4 leaves). The first sheet consists of 2 blank leaves, the half-title, and the frontis-piece: pages 1 to 111 are occupied by *John Ball,*—113 to 123 by *A King's Lesson.* The half-title and colophon are

(106)

A DREAM OF JOHN BALL AND
A KING'S LESSON. BY WILLIAM
MORRIS.

[Over the colophon is the smaller book-mark.]

This book, a Dream of John Ball and a King's/ Lesson, was written by William Morris, and/ printed by him at the Kelmscott Press, Upper/ Mall, Hammersmith, in the County of Middle-/sex ; and finished on the 13th day of May, 1892./ Sold by Reeves & Turner, 196, Strand, London.

The first page of each story is surrounded by an ornamental border of the author's designing. The type is the golden-type. The style of get-up as usual, with red shoulder-notes in lieu of head-lines, ornamental capitals of two sizes by Morris, a limp vellum binding with complete sheets for end-papers, silk ties, and the title "JOHN/ BALL" lettered in gold across the back.

In 1888 Morris was aiding in the establishment of the Arts and Crafts Exhibition Society; and the catalogue of their first exhibition contains an essay by him on Textiles. His great work of this year, however, is *The House of the Wolfings*, which was not only written but completely printed by the end of the year (though dated 1889),—1000 copies on ordinary paper, square crown 8vo. (imperial 16mo.), by the 15th of December, and 100 on large paper (hand-made, crown quarto) by the 31st of the same month. When the book had just passed through the press all but the title-page and other pre-liminary leaves, it chanced that I had business at the Chiswick Press; and there I fell in with Morris, come in person to have his way about his title-page and settle final points. He called my attention to the peculiarities of the old fount of type which had been used for the book, answered a few questions about the scheme of this new departure in literature, and seemed to be as hearty and full of creative go and enthusiasm as ever. Pre-sently down came the proof of the title-page. It did not read quite as now: the difference, I think, was in the fourth and fifth lines where the words stood " written in prose and verse by William Morris." Now unhappily the words and the type did not so accord as to come up to Morris's standard of decora-tiveness. The line wanted tightening up: there was a three-cornered consultation between the Author, the Manager, and myself. The word *in* was to be inserted—" written in prose and *in* verse "—to gain the necessary fulness of line. I mildly protested that the former reading was the better sense and that it should not be sacrificed to avoid a slight excess of white that no one would notice. " Ha!" said Morris, " now what would you say if I told you that the verses on the title-page were written just to fill up the great white lower half? Well that was what happened!" And here is the title-page about which so much high energy was liberated :—

(107)

A TALE OF THE HOUSE OF THE
WOLFINGS AND ALL THE KIND-
REDS OF THE MARK WRITTEN
IN PROSE AND IN VERSE
BY WILLIAM MORRIS.

WHILES IN THE EARLY WINTER EVE
WE PASS AMID THE GATHERING NIGHT
SOME HOMESTEAD THAT WE HAD TO LEAVE
YEARS PAST; AND SEE ITS CANDLES BRIGHT
SHINE IN THE ROOM BESIDE THE DOOR
WHERE WE WERE MERRY YEARS AGONE
BUT NOW MUST NEVER ENTER MORE,
AS STILL THE DARK ROAD DRIVES US ON.
E'EN SO THE WORLD OF MEN MAY TURN
AT EVEN OF SOME HURRIED DAY
AND SEE THE ANCIENT GLIMMER BURN
ACROSS THE WASTE THAT HATH NO WAY;
THEN WITH THAT FAINT LIGHT IN ITS EYES
A WHILE I BID IT LINGER NEAR
AND NURSE IN WAVERING MEMORIES
THE BITTER-SWEET OF DAYS THAT WERE.

LONDON 1889: REEVES AND TURNER 196 STRAND.

The volume consists of four preliminary leaves and 200 pages of the story itself. The first leaf is blank but for the signature, A, the second is the half-title ("THE HOUSE OF THE WOLFINGS."), the third the title with imprint on verso, "CHISWICK PRESS:—CHARLES WHITTINGHAM AND CO./ TOOKS COURT, CHANCERY LANE.", the fourth the table of contents, one page. The arrangement of the page is the ordinary modern one,—Arabic numbering in the outer top corners, head-lines on all versos "THE HOUSE OF THE WOLFINGS," and on rectos subject head-lines. The ordinary copies were put up in unblocked dark red cloth and the large-paper in cherry-coloured buckram. Both have printed back-labels, the ordinary reading "The House/ of the/ Wolfings/ William/ Morris/ *Price 6s.*"; and the large-paper copies contain a certificate: "One hundred copies of this Large Paper Edition have been printed, of which Eighty-nine were for sale." This is on a slip, pasted on to the first end-paper. The quaint fount of type used for this book was cut by one Howard some half-century ago, and is but little known. The page was set with an eye to the ordinary copies; and the large-paper copies, which are very handsome, have far more margin than the master-printer of the Kelmscott Press would have tolerated a year or two later.   Indeed the next book showed repentance in the matter of margin.

The Roots of the Mountains, the pendant in many regards of *The House of the Wolfings*, conceived in the same spirit, set in the same type, with its title-page modelled on the same lines, was made and devised, so far as typography is concerned, with an eye to the very choice large-paper copies.   The paper, thin and tough, was manufactured especially for this work, of pot-size; and the special edition is a pot quarto.   The ordinary copies are square crown 8vo. (imperial 16mo.).   But before the title is set out it must be recorded that it appeared first as page 1 of a small hand-bill of two leaves, the first (108) leaf announcing this work, and the second advertizing others.   This hand-bill is the first issue of the poem on the following title-page :—

(109)

THE ROOTS OF THE MOUNTAINS
WHEREIN IS TOLD SOMEWHAT OF
THE LIVES OF THE MEN OF BURG/
DALE   THEIR   FRIENDS   THEIR
NEIGHBOURS THEIR FOEMEN AND
THEIR FELLOWS IN ARMS
BY WILLIAM MORRIS

WHILES CARRIED O'ER THE IRON ROAD,
WE HURRY BY SOME FAIR ABODE ;
THE GARDEN BRIGHT AMIDST THE HAY,
THE YELLOW WAIN UPON THE WAY,
THE DINING MEN, THE WIND THAT SWEEPS
LIGHT LOCKS FROM OFF THE SUN-SWEET HEAPS—
THE GABLE GREY, THE HOARY ROOF,
HERE NOW—AND NOW SO FAR ALOOF.
HOW SORELY THEN WE LONG TO STAY
AND MIDST ITS SWEETNESS WEAR THE DAY,
AND 'NEATH ITS CHANGING SHADOWS SIT,
AND FEEL OURSELVES A PART OF IT.
SUCH REST, SUCH STAY, I STROVE TO WIN,
WITH THESE SAME LEAVES THAT LIE HEREIN.

LONDON MDCCCXC: REEVES AND TURNER
CXCVI STRAND

The preliminary leaves are four, one having the signature A on the recto and a certificate on the verso in the special edition, but an advertizement of Morris's books in the ordinary edition, a half-title ("THE ROOTS OF THE MOUNTAINS"), the title with Whittingham's imprint on the verso, and a list of contents occupying two pages ; and the Story occupies 424 pages. Here "dropped heads," head-lines, and numbering in the top corners were abandoned. The equivalents of head-lines are given in side-notes at the top of the outer margins ; and the pages are centrally numbered at the foot in Arabic figures. The certificate reads thus :—" Of this, the superior edition on Whatman paper, only two hundred and fifty copies are printed. Charles Whittingham and Co." Even hereby hangs a tale : for when Morris announced his intention of having 250 copies on Whatman's paper, one of his consultants said, "Why, that's an edition,—not large-paper copies !"— "Well," said Morris, "then hang it ! call it an edition." And an edition it was called. It will be noticed that the title-page is more decoratively arranged than that of *The Wolfings ;* and that the publication lines are got quite right by substituting a date in Roman figures for that in Arabic figures. The special edition was done up in two sorts of Morris & Co.'s chintz, one of a large pattern and the other of a small, both lettered in gold on the back "The/ Roots/ of the/ Mountains/ William/ Morris." The ordinary issue was bound in dark red cloth, unblocked ; and the legend was affixed to the back by means of a printed label reading "THE/ ROOTS/ OF THE/ MOUN-TAINS/ WILLIAM MORRIS/ *Price* 6s." In the ordinary copies a catalogue of Reeves & Turner's publications (32 pages) is inserted at the end : the catalogue was printed by Messrs. Bowden, Hudson & Co., of Red Lion Street.

The charming little poem which fills up the "central waste" of the title-page reflects an incident of real life. Morris was journeying by railway through the country with Mr. Emery Walker the summer before the book came out. They passed by "the iron road" through meadows where hay-making was toward, and saw the hay-cocks defrauded by the summer breeze. "There !" said Mr. Walker, "A subject for your title-page, Morris !" "Aye," said Morris ; and the subject was jotted down in pencil in one of the books (four of them) which contain the complete first draft of the romance. This volume treads upon the threshold of the Kelmscott Press in the matter of style, though not touching upon the decorative splendour of that press. It is a connecting link in another way between the Chiswick and Kelmscott Presses. Of this Whatman paper, Morris had to buy "the whole making." There was a lot over. When he set up his own press to print books on his own water-marked paper, he took the remainder of that redundant "making" with him; and it is on that that the first little post quarto catalogues and prospectuses were printed at Hammersmith. But there are still a few matters to be disposed of before we come by the proper road of bibliographical chronology to the Kelmscott Press; for the main stream of this book is the stream of *editiones principes ;* and the Kelmscott Press has only so far come into the tale because of its reprints of *editiones principes.*

Before the Socialist League broke up, *The Socialist Platform* was increased by one number of which the title-page is—

(110)

"The Socialist Platform."— No. 7.

MONOPOLY ;

OR,

HOW LABOUR IS ROBBED. .

BY

WILLIAM MORRIS

AUTHOR OF 'THE EARTHLY PARADISE.'

PRICE ONE PENNY.

LONDON:
OFFICE OF "THE COMMONWEAL"
24 GREAT QUEEN STREET, LINCOLN'S INN FIELDS, W.C.
1890.

This is a crown 8vo. sheet trimmed at the bottom and fore-
edge and fastened with a single metal fastener. On the verso
of the title is a hideous cartoon. The text ends on page 15,
at the foot of which is the imprint "SOCIALIST LEAGUE
PRINTERS, 24 GREAT QUEEN STREET, W.C." Page 16 is full of
       Socialist advertizements. There is a reïssue of the
(111)   whole series, including the Manifesto and the Chants,
       with an enlarged "Contents" to take in *Monopoly*,
and a title varying from No. 103 as to date and address.
Also it has a sort of mottled terra-cotta-coloured wrapper
instead of a green one. The imprint both on title and on
wrapper is "LONDON :/ OFFICE OF 'THE COMMON-
WEAL,'/ 24, GREAT QUEEN STREET, LINCOLN'S INN FIELDS,
W.C./ 1890./ *Price One Shilling.*" *Monopoly* was
(112)   reprinted in 1893 by the Hammersmith Socialist
       Society, with Mr. Crane's Labour and Justice design
on the title-page.

In the Arts and Crafts Catalogue of 1889 there was an
essay by Morris on Dyeing as an Art : in that for 1890 there
was no essay by him ; but there were two by his daughter
May, connected with his on Dyeing. Here, as in the Socialist
movement, she was coöperating with her father ; and much
beautiful work of hers has been exhibited by the Society. It
was in this year 1890 that the " Branch "—the Hammersmith
Branch of the Socialist League—parted with its " Flower " in
the sense recorded at page 136 of this volume ; it was in this
year that the Branch itself ceased to be a Branch and became
the Hammersmith Socialist Society on the disruption of the
League. As the year drew to a close the differences between the
members of the League became so irreconcileable that Morris
practically withdrew from participation in *The Commonweal ;*
but he allowed his *News from Nowhere*, which was appearing in
the columns of the paper, to be finished there. The conclusion
appeared in the number for the 4th of October. Morris did
not intend to wait long before revising it and issuing it in a
popular form to show Mr. Bellamy's many admirers how that
kind of work should be done. But before the artist's revision
of the work was complete, Messrs. Roberts Brothers of Boston
in Massachusetts reprinted it unrevised from *The Commonweal*,
and so produced an *editio princeps* which has not the advantage
of the author's finishing touches. Its title-page is as follows :—

(113)

NEWS FROM NOWHERE ;

OR,

An Epoch of Rest.

BEING SOME CHAPTERS FROM A UTOPIAN ROMANCE.

BY

WILLIAM MORRIS,

AUTHOR OF "THE EARTHLY PARADISE," "THE LIFE AND DEATH OF JASON," "THE DEFENCE OF GUENEVERE AND OTHER POEMS," "LOVE IS ENOUGH," "THE STORY OF SIGURD THE VOLSUNG," "THE HOUSE OF THE WOLFINGS," "HOPES AND FEARS FOR ART," "THE AENEIDS OF VIRGIL DONE INTO ENGLISH VERSE."

[device]

BOSTON :

ROBERTS BROTHERS.

1890.

This crown 8vo. volume has a half-title reading " NEWS FROM NOWHERE ;/ OR,/ AN EPOCH OF REST." On the verso Mr. Crane's cartoon, "Labour's May-Day," is printed as a frontispiece, reduced to the size here indicated. On the verso of the title are the words *" Author's Edition "* and the imprint "University Press :/ JOHN WILSON AND SON, CAMBRIDGE." The " Contents " occupy pages v and vi and the text pages 7 to 278. The head-lines are, verso, " NEWS FROM NOWHERE," and recto, " OR, AN EPOCH OF REST." After p. 278 are two pages of advertizements of Morris's works and an eight-page reprint of an article from *The Athenæum* on *The House of the Wolfings.* This first edition of *News from Nowhere* was issued in cloth with the edges trimmed round. By Morris's permission I obtained two unbound copies for binding with the edges untrimmed. I am unable to say what the binding of 1890 was like. At present the Boston edition, dated 1894, is (114) in dark red cloth lettered in grey on the front cover, in the centre of which is a terrestrial hemisphere stamped in gold with the legend " Solidarity of labour " across it. I do not understand the words " Author's Edition "; nor

LABOUR'S MAY-DAY.

CARTOON BY WALTER CRANE, AS REDUCED FOR THE FRONTISPIECE OF THE
(AMERICAN) EDITIO PRINCEPS OF "NEWS FROM NOWHERE."

10—2

did Morris, who first showed me the book and told me with an amused air that he had not been consulted about it. Morris's own first edition did not come out till the spring of 1891, when it appeared in three forms. Being meant for popular reading, the main issue was but a thick trimmed pamphlet in a paper wrapper; but those who liked to have it in dark bottle-green cloth uncut, could by paying a few pence extra. Then there was a large-paper issue printed on a pretty French hand-made paper, tall crown 8vo., in blue paper boards with Japanese paper backs and printed labels reading " NEWS/ from/ NO-WHERE/ by/ William Morris/ Large Paper." Of this three-fold issue the title is—

(115)

NEWS FROM NOWHERE

OR

AN EPOCH OF REST,

BEING SOME CHAPTERS FROM

A UTOPIAN ROMANCE

BY

WILLIAM MORRIS

AUTHOR OF THE EARTHLY PARADISE.

LONDON:

REEVES & TURNER.

1891.

There are 238 pages, numbered in the outer corners but with-out head-lines. The title is a single leaf with a blank verso. In the hand-made copies is a certificate printed on the 4th page of a quarter-sheet (2 leaves) and reading " *This Large Paper Edition of ' News from Nowhere '/ is limited to Two Hundred and Fifty copies.*" There is no printer's name; but I believe the book was printed at a small transpontine press by a Mr. Bowden. Copies of the ordinary book measure $7\frac{1}{8}$ inches by a shade over $4\frac{1}{2}$. By special favour of Mr. Reeves I have one uncut with the wrapper : it measures $7\frac{9}{16} \times 5$. The wrapper reads " News from Nowhere/ BY/ WILLIAM MORRIS,/

AUTHOR OF 'THE EARTHLY PARADISE,' ETC./ LONDON :/ REEVES & TURNER, 196, STRAND./ MDCCCXCI./ *One Shilling.*" It is on the same mottled terra-cotta-coloured paper as the cover of the completed issue of *The Socialist Platform.* In the following year the book was raised to the dignity of an 8vo. Kelmscott impression, in the golden type, with all the luxury of limp vellum binding with silk ties and half-sheet end-papers, and bold lettering of gold, " NEWS/ FROM/ NOWHERE/ BY/ WILLIAM/ MORRIS." The undated title or half-title, whichever the expert may be pleased to call it, is as follows :—

(116)

NEWS FROM NOWHERE: OR,
AN EPOCH OF REST, BEING SOME
CHAPTERS FROM A UTOPIAN RO-
MANCE, BY WILLIAM MORRIS.

The colophon reads thus :—

> This book, News from Nowhere or an Epoch/ of Rest, was written by William Morris, and/ printed by him at the Kelmscott Press, Upper/ Mall, Hammersmith, in the County of Middle-/sex, and finished on the 22nd day of November,/ 1892. Sold by Reeves & Turner, 196, Strand,/ London.
>   [the lesser book-mark.]

Of 4 preliminary leaves (sig. A) one is blank, the second is the title with blank verso, the third " A list of the Chapters of this Book " (on both sides), and the fourth a delightful frontispiece with blank recto. The frontispiece, cut on wood in broad line from a drawing by Mr. Gere, represents Kelmscott Manor. There is a border by Morris, and an inscription, in golden type capitals, reading "This is the picture of the old house by the Thames to which the people of this story went. Hereafter follows the book itself which is called News from Nowhere or an Epoch of Rest & is written by William Morris." And on the opposite page the book begins within a grape-vine border. There are 305 pages of it, with shoulder-notes in red in lieu of headlines, and with ornamental capitals galore. Page 305 is the first of a half-sheet : the colophon is on page 306 ; and the other three leaves are blanks additional to the end-papers.

The bottom and fore-edge are trimmed. It is worth men-
tioning that, in 1895, *News from Nowhere* was printed
(117)   in Italian at Milan under the title *La Terra Promessa.*
It was translated by Ernestina d'Errico, and has an
amusing introduction and notes.

The standing of an *editio princeps* must presumably be
assigned to the tiny pamphlet with the following title :—

(118)

THE LEGEND

OF

"The Briar Rose."

A SERIES OF PICTURES

PAINTED BY

E. BURNE JONES, A.R.A.

EXHIBITED AT

THOS. AGNEW & SONS' GALLERIES,
39, OLD BOND STREET, W.
1890.

These six demy 16mo. leaves sewn together through the middle
were sold or given to people who went to see the mar-
vellous Briar Rose pictures. There is a half-title, " THE
LEGEND/ OF/ 'The Briar Rose.'" The verso is blank :
so is that of the title-page. Pages 5 to 9 contain the legend
in prose. Pages 10 and 11 are occupied by Morris's four
quatrains. Page 12 advertizes photogravures of the pictures.

Before the exhibition closed an extended pamphlet
(119)   of 24 pages, foolscap 8vo., was on sale at the gallery
for sixpence in a grey wrapper. The prose text is
different from that of the other ; and Morris's quatrains are
placed as headings to the descriptions of the pictures by
E. J. Milliken. From these pamphlets in which Morris's
name is connected with one of his oldest and most distinguished friends, we pass, curiously enough, to one which
reflects a breaking-up. The Socialist League gives place to
the Hammersmith Socialist Society ; and there is a new manifesto, again of Morris's writing :—

(120)

Statement of Principles of the Hammersmith Socialist Society

PUBLISHED BY THE SOCIETY AT KELMSCOTT HOUSE, UPPER MALL, HAMMERSMITH, W.

PRICE ONE PENNY.

This is a crown 8vo. pamphlet of eight pages, stitched through the fold and without a wrapper. On the verso of the title are the rules of the society. Page 3 starts with an ordinary dropped head repeating the title in roman type. Pages 4 to 8 are numbered centrally in Arabic figures. The last paragraph is followed by the date " December, 1890." At the foot, below a thin rule, is the imprint " Co-operative Printing Society Limited, 6, Salisbury Court, Fleet Street, and/ 35, Russell Street, Covent Garden, London. (15,183.)" At about the same time Morris was contributing to *The New Review* an article on the Socialist Ideal in Art. It appeared in the number for January 1891, and was reprinted as an untrimmed crown 8vo. pamphlet of 12 pages all told, fastened with a single wire fastener. The title-page is as follows :—

(121)

THE SOCIALIST IDEAL OF ART.

BY

WILLIAM MORRIS,

*AUTHOR OF " THE EARTHLY PARADISE,"
" A DREAM OF JOHN BALL," " NEWS FROM
NOWHERE," &c. &c.*

———•‡❉‡•———

LONDON :
REPRINTED FROM "THE NEW REVIEW,"
JANUARY, 1891.

The verso is blank. There are no head-lines or imprint. The pages are numbered centrally in Arabic figures.

THE KELMSCOTT PRESS

AND THE EDITIONES PRINCIPES
ISSUED FROM IT.

The story of the Glittering Plain or the Land of Living Men

Reduced copy of Design by Morris for the quarto edition of "The Glittering Plain" illustrated by Walter Crane.

THE KELMSCOTT PRESS:

ALTHOUGH this is not the occasion on which to write the history of the Kelmscott Press, the point in our bibliographical chronology has now been reached, at which Morris threw off the oppression of the modern printers and issued his books from a plain house represented in the accompanying picture, — No. 14, Upper Mall, Hammersmith, where his founts of type, his blocks, his hand presses and the rest, still abide for awhile. The first book issued from the Kelmscott Press was his own wonderful romance, *The Glittering Plain*, which had appeared in *The English Illustrated Magazine*. Though the shape is that of an octavo, the book may be described as a quarto; for it is not only printed in fours, but each four leaves go to make up a complete little sheet with deckel edges all round. It starts with the signature a on an otherwise blank leaf. Signature a2 is at the foot of the title-page, which reads thus :—

(122)

THE STORY OF THE GLITTERING
PLAIN. WHICH HAS BEEN ALSO
CALLED THE LAND OF LIVING
MEN OR THE ACRE OF THE UN-
DYING. WRITTEN BY WILLIAM
MORRIS.

On the verso is " A Table of the Chapters of this Book." The
first page of the text is surrounded by a beautiful border
designed by Morris, filling almost entirely what is margin in
the ordinary pages. This is a part of the system of the Kelmscott books—marginal decoration. There are 187 pages of the
story ; and at the top of page 188 is the colophon—

HERE endeth the Glittering Plain, printed by/ William
Morris at the Kelmscott Press, Up-/per Mall Hammersmith, in the County of/ Middlesex : and finished on the
4th day of/ April of the year 1891./ Sold by Reeves &
Turner 196 Strand London.

The ornamental initials for the chapters are an inch and three
quarters square,—those for sections of chapters a little over an
inch square. Paragraphs, minor divisions, parts of the dialogue
&c. are marked by an old-fashioned paragraph-sign, which is a
little obtrusive in its blackness, and of which the use was
abandoned. The book is printed in the golden type, without
either head-lines or side-notes, and the pages are numbered at
the foot with Arabic figures. The binding is of vellum with
stiff boards and chamois leather ties. The end papers are complete sheets of a paper similar to but not identical with that
used for the book. The back is lettered in gold capitals " THE/
STORY/ OF/ THE/ GLIT-/ TER-/ ING/ PLAIN/ BY/
WILL-/ IAM/ MORRIS/ 1891." Two hundred copies were
printed; but only one hundred and eighty were offered for sale,
at two guineas each. There were six vellum copies. The issue
was subscribed for at once; and the book is difficult to get. Of
course an edition for the general public was immediately forth-
coming. Its title is as follows :—

(123)

THE STORY OF THE GLITTER-/ ING PLAIN WHICH
HAS BEEN/ ALSO CALLED THE LAND OF/ LIVING
MEN OR THE ACRE OF/ THE UNDYING WRITTEN/
BY WILLIAM MORRIS/ LONDON : REEVES AND
TURNER/ MDCCCXCI

A page of advertizements, half-title, title, list of contents and
172 pages of text are bound up in an Imperial 16mo. volume in
dark green cloth lettered in gold on the front cover and at the
back. The title-page which Morris designed for this book when
it was reprinted in quarto with Mr. Crane's illustrations is
placed at the beginning of this section as being one of the finest
of his Kelmscott designs. The half-title and colophon of that
beautiful volume, printed in black and red in the Troy type,
are as follows :—

(124)

THE STORY OF THE GLITTERING PLAIN BY
WILLIAM MORRIS

Here ends the tale of the Glittering Plain, written by
William Morris & ornamented with 23 pictures by
Walter Crane. Printed at the Kelmscott Press, Upper
Mall, Hammersmith, in the County of Middlesex, &
finished on the 13th day of January 1894

This book, bound in limp vellum with silk ties, has the usual
allowance of end-papers and preliminary leaves. The ornamental title is a verso—in fact a frontispiece. The text occupies
pages 1 to 177 ; and at the end is the larger Kelmscott mark.
The impression was 250 copies on paper and 7 on
(125) vellum. The story in a plain form is now to be had
of Messrs. Longmans with a fresh title substituting
their address for that of Messrs. Reeves and Turner.
Concerning *Poems by the Way*, the next *editio princeps* from
the Press, there is a better tale to tell than that of the Verses
written to fill up the title-page of *The House of the Wolfings*.
Before the summer of 1891 it had been determined to issue
from the Kelmscott Press a new volume of Poems by Morris.
On the 16th of June he wrote to his publishers that he should
print 250 copies, in black and red, and that, if it came out

smaller than *The Glittering Plain*, it must be sold at a lower price : on the other hand, if it came out larger, the price should still not exceed two guineas ; so it was to be announced forthwith as a two guinea book of the same *format* as *The Glittering Plain*. When the book had been set up in type as far as page 166, the measure seemed to the author to be short. He said to Mr. Emery Walker that he thought he would write something to plump the volume out a bit: it was morning when this took place ; and in the evening of the same day he produced a new Manuscript poem and read it to Mr. Walker. This was no other than the delightful poem *Goldilocks and Goldilocks* forming the last thirty pages of *Poems by the Way*, —a poem full of the spirit of his later prose romances and especially recalling to the mind *The Roots of the Mountains* and *The Well at the World's End*, but written in four-foot anapæstic couplets of such a fresh and spring-like impulse that it is a matter worthy of all regret that he did not oftener find himself driven to verse these latter years. This second of his Kelmscott books is a small quarto of crown 8vo. appearance, untrimmed, bound in vellum with silk ties, and lettered across the back "POEMS/ BY/ THE/ WAY/ BY/ WILL-/ IAM/ MORRIS/ 1891." The first leaf bears at the top the words

(126)

POEMS BY THE WAY. WRITTEN
BY WILLIAM MORRIS.

The second leaf contains "A Table of the Contents of this Book," as follows :—

The text fills pages 1 to 196, starting with an ornamental border, and continuing with a wealth of decorative initials great and small, and rubricated as to shoulder-notes and refrains. The colophon, on page 197, is

HERE endeth Poems by the Way, written/ by William Morris, and printed by him at the/ Kelmscott Press, Upper Mall, Hammersmith,/ in the County of Middlesex; and finished on/ the 24th day of September of the year 1891./ Sold by Reeves & Turner, 196, Strand, London.

The lesser book-mark follows; the verso is blank; and there is a blank leaf beside the usual full-sheet (4 leaves) endpapers.

It was not to be supposed that the short issue of the Kelmscott Press would suffice to meet the needs of the reading public; and the *editio princeps* was accordingly followed at once by an edition printed at the Chiswick Press with the following title:—

(127)

POEMS BY THE WAY/ WRITTEN BY WILLIAM/ MORRIS/ LONDON: REEVES AND TURNER/ MDCCCXCI

This is an Imperial 16mo. consisting of 196 pages of poetry and four preliminary leaves. The first has a blank recto but for the signature A, and on the verso are advertizements of Morris's books; the second is a half-title, *Poems by the Way;* the third is the title with a blank verso; and the fourth is a two-page list of contents printed in italics. Page 1 opens with the quaint " Here begin " &c. as the Kelmscott edition does; and the system of *The Roots of the Mountains* is adopted, —no dropped heads or head-lines, titles at the tops of the outer margins, and Arabic numerals at the foot of the page. The book is bound in unblocked dark-green cloth, and gilt-lettered at the back. Large paper copies on hand-made paper, post quarto, were printed and numbered in Manuscript. The certificate is on the verso of signature A1, instead of the advertizements, and reads " *Only One Hundred copies printed. This is No.....*" These copies are choicely printed and most agreeable to read. They are bound in cream-white buckram, unblocked, gilt-lettered at the back " POEMS/ BY/ THE WAY/ WILLIAM/ MORRIS/ REEVES/ &/ TURNER." The front cover is gilt-lettered " POEMS BY THE WAY/ WRITTEN BY WILLIAM/ MORRIS." *Poems by* (128) *the Way* and *Love is Enough* (not very suitable companions) now form one volume in that nice set of books which Messrs. Longmans sell in ten volumes labelled as The Poetical Works of William Morris.

Next to his own collection of shorter poems Morris printed The Love Lyrics, Songs, and Sonnets of " Proteus " (Wilfrid Scawen Blunt), finished in black and red (the ornamented capitals in red) on the 26th of January 1892; but here he appears simply as printer and decorator; and the collector of his literary works has nothing to do with this volume. Meanwhile he had begun a big undertaking in another way.

(129)

THE SAGA LIBRARY.

VOL. I.

THE STORY OF HOWARD THE HALT.
THE STORY OF THE BANDED MEN.
THE STORY OF HEN THORIR.

DONE INTO ENGLISH
OUT OF THE ICELANDIC.

BY

WILLIAM MORRIS

AND

EIRÍKR MAGNÚSSON.

LONDON:
BERNARD QUARITCH, 15 PICCADILLY.
1891.

This, like other volumes of the Saga Library, is a crown 8vo.
printed upon a thinnish creamy laid paper with false deckel
edges. It has a half-title "THE SAGA LIBRARY," a title,
pages v to xlvii of preface, a second half-title for *Howard the
Halt*, a leaf with four lines of *corrigenda*, a map, and 227
pages of text, notes, etc. The Chiswick Press imprint appears
both on the verso of the title and at the foot of page 227. The
head-lines are in upper and lower case italics, "*The Saga
Library*" on versos and the name of the particular tale or
section on rectos. The book is half bound in an ornamented
Roxburgh style, dark green leather backs and sage-green cloth
sides. The lettering is, at the back, "THE/ SAGA/ LIBRARY/
VOL. I./ HOWARD/ THE/ HALT/ WILLIAM/ MORRIS,"
and on the side, "HOWARD THE HALT/ THE BANDED
MEN/ HEN THORIR." The ornaments are sprays of foliage
designed by Morris. The books were delivered in grey paper
wrappers on which the back and side designs are printed in
black. There are large-paper copies, hand-made demy 8vo.,
bound in the same style.

There are also some pamphlets belonging to the year 1891 :—

(130)

CITY OF BIRMINGHAM
MUSEUM AND ART GALLERY.

[Arms.]

ADDRESS
ON THE
COLLECTION OF PAINTINGS,
OF THE
ENGLISH PRE-RAPHAELITE SCHOOL,

DELIVERED BY
MR. WILLIAM MORRIS,

IN THE MUSEUM AND ART GALLERY,
ON FRIDAY, OCTOBER 2ND, 1891.

BIRMINGHAM :
E. C. OSBORNE AND SON, 84, NEW STREET.
PRICE ONE PENNY.

This is a single sheet demy 8vo. trimmed and wire-stitched, without head-lines but with pages 4 to 16 numbered centrally in Arabic figures.

(131)

PRICE ONE PENNY.

Under an Elm-Tree;

Or, Thoughts in the Country-Side. By Wm. Morris, Author of "The Earthly Paradise," &c. &c.

Aberdeen :
PRINTED AND PUBLISHED BY JAMES LEATHAM,
15 ST. NICHOLAS STREET.

1891.

This is a sixteen-page pamphlet, demy 16mo., stitched through the middle, uncut. It was sold without a wrapper; but special copies are occasionally found with a pale green printed wrapper added, bearing the words "𝔘𝔫𝔡𝔢𝔯 𝔞𝔫 𝔈𝔩𝔪=𝔱𝔯𝔢𝔢 ;/ *Or, Thoughts in the/ Country-Side. By/ Wm. Morris.*"

(132)

Reprinted in this form by the kind permission of Messrs. Reeves & Turner, Publishers of Mr. Morris' Works.

A KING'S LESSON

BY

WILLIAM MORRIS

Author of " The Earthly Paradise," etc.

𝔄𝔟𝔢𝔯𝔡𝔢𝔢𝔫 :
PRINTED AND PUBLISHED BY JAMES LEATHAM
15 ST. NICHOLAS STREET
1891.

This too is a sixteen-page 16mo. pamphlet, but trimmed and in a grey printed wrapper.

In February 1892 came out

(133)

THE NATURE OF GOTHIC A CHAP-/ TER OF THE STONES OF VENICE./ BY JOHN RUSKIN.

Here the collector of Morris's works is concerned. It is one of the " small quartos " of the early days of the press, printed in the golden type, in black only, and bound in vellum with silk ties and the usual eight-page end-papers. The book starts with a blank leaf; on the verso of the half-title given above begins a five-page preface by Morris, signed and dated on the verso of the 4th leaf, and followed by the lesser book-mark. Page 1 has a decorative border and large initial. There are 128 pages of text, with a few illustrations of Ruskin's as well as Morris's initial letters. The colophon is

HERE ends the Nature of Gothic, by John Rus-/ kin, printed by William Morris at the Kelmscott/ Press, Hammersmith, and published by George/ Allen, 8, Bell Yard, Temple Bar, London, and/ Sunnyside, Orpington.

The lesser book-mark ends the volume. The Kelmscott prints of *The Defence of Guenevere* and *John Ball*, which followed, have already been described. Next came Caxton's *Golden Legend*, edited by Mr. F. S. Ellis and published by Mr. Quaritch—three thick quarto volumes ; but here again Morris as author is not concerned unless it be in the colophon   *The Recuyell of the Historyes of Troye* and the *Biblia Innocentium* followed without Morris's participation save as printer,—then, still in 1892, the Kelmscott *News from Nowhere*, already described, and Caxton's *History of Reynard the Foxe*, with one of Morris's finest designed titles. Meanwhile the second volume of the Saga Library came out—

(134)

THE STORY OF THE ERE-DWELLERS

(EYRBYGGJA SAGA)

WITH

THE STORY OF THE HEATH-SLAYINGS

(HEIÐARVIGA SAGA)

AS APPENDIX

DONE INTO ENGLISH
OUT OF THE ICELANDIC

BY

WILLIAM MORRIS

AND

EIRÍKR MAGNÚSSON

LONDON
BERNARD QUARITCH, 15 PICCADILLY
1892

In this volume the half-title is extended—"THE SAGA LIBRARY/ EDITED BY/ WILLIAM MORRIS/ AND/ EIRÍKR MAGNÚSSON/ VOL. II./ EYRBYGGJA SAGA." The book has lii + 410 pages, with a map, a corrigenda-leaf, and an imprint-leaf at the end.

The Kelmscott Press began the year 1893 with an 8vo. edition of Shakespeare's Poems in the golden type, edited by Mr. Ellis, who also co-öperated with his old friend in the next

(135) book to be described,—*The Order of Chivalry* and *The Ordination of Knighthood.* This 8vo. volume, bound in limp vellum with silk ties and lettered in gold up the back "THE ORDER OF CHIVALRY," also starts with a page bearing those words only. On the verso of the leaf begins the quaint "Table of this present booke Intytled The Book of the Ordre of Chyualry or Knyghthode." This table ends on the recto of the frontispiece by Sir Edward Burne-Jones, which, having in a flowered compartment beneath it and within the same border by Morris the words "The/ Order of/ Chivalry," may serve as title-page. The Caxton text of 1484 follows in the Chaucer type, on pages 1 to 101. On page 102 is the colophon (followed by the lesser book-mark)—

> The Order of Chivalry, translated from/ the French by William Caxton, edited by/ F. S. Ellis, and printed by me William Morris/ at the Kelmscott Press, Upper Mall, Ham-/ mersmith, in the County of Middlesex &/ finished on the 10th day of November, 1892/ Sold by Reeves & Turner, 196, Strand,/ London.

Pages 103, 104 and 106 are blank, 105 having the half-title "L'ORDENE DE CHEVALERIE, WITH/ TRANSLATION BY WILLIAM MORRIS." The French poem occupies pages 107 to 125; 126 is blank; on 127 is the half-title "THE ORDINATION OF KNIGHTHOOD"; and Morris's version in short couplets occupies pages 128 to 147. On 148 to 151 are Mr. Ellis's memoranda: the following colophon and the lesser book-mark complete 151 : 152 is blank:

> THIS Ordination of Knighthood was/ printed by William Morris at the Kelms-/ cott Press, Upper Mall, Hammer-/ smith,/ in the County of Middlesex; finished on/ the 24th day of February, 1893.

In March and April followed Cavendish's Life of Wolsey, edited by Mr. Ellis from the Manuscript in the British Museum, and Caxton's *Godeffroye of Boloyne* edited by Mr. Sparling. In May Morris was concerned in the writing of another manifesto,—that of the Joint Committee of Socialist Bodies,—an 8vo. pamphlet of 8 pages, numbered centrally, and with no title-page save what is outside a blood-red wrapper, namely

(136)

MANIFESTO

OF

ENGLISH
SOCIALISTS

PRICE ONE PENNY.

MAY 1, 1893.

Printed by the Twentieth Century Press Limited, 44, Gray's Inn Road, Holborn, W.C.

This he wrote conjointly with Mr. H. M. Hyndman and Mr. George Bernard Shaw. Meantime the publication of pamphlets by the Hammersmith Socialist Society was going on; and we must here set down the details of an undated one reprinted from *The Commonweal*, a trimmed crown 8vo. of 12 pages with no title save that on the Turner-grey wrapper, which is—

(137)

THE REWARD OF LABOUR: A DIALOGUE BY WILLIAM MORRIS, AUTHOR OF "THE EARTHLY PARADISE."

BEING No. 1 OF THE HAMMERSMITH SOCIALIST LIBRARY.

ONE PENNY

At the foot of page 12 is the imprint (below a thin rule) "HAYMAN, CHRISTY & LILLY, LTD., PRINTERS, 20 & 22 ST. BRIDE ST., E.C." On the 4th page of the wrapper is an advertizement. In the catalogue of the sixth summer exhibition at the New Gallery (page 16) are four couplets for Sir Edward Burne-Jones's two pictures of the Romance of the Rose; and in the same summer the "Anti-Scrape" had a substantive contribution from Morris, a crown 8vo. pamphlet of a single sheet, which was distributed by the Society without any wrapper, and without the author's name, but which also occurs in a smooth grey wrapper. The title-page is—

(138)

THE

SOCIETY FOR THE PROTECTION OF ANCIENT BUILDINGS.

CONCERNING

WESTMINSTER ABBEY.

LONDON

9, Buckingham Street, Adelphi, W.C.

The verso of the title is blank. The text is on pages 3 to 14 without head-lines, numbered centrally in Arabic figures. At the foot of page 14, below a thin rule, is the imprint, "Women's Printing Society, Ltd., 66, Whitcomb Street, W.C." Pages 15 and 16 are blank. On the wrapper, beside the first five lines of the title-page, arranged in colophon form, are the words "*LONDON: JUNE, 1893/* [250 Copies for the Author/ WILLIAM MORRIS."] Two months later his edition of More's *Utopia* was through the Kelmscott Press,—an 8vo. printed in the Chaucer type in black and red, bound in limp vellum with silk ties, lettered in gold across the back "MORE'S/ UTOPIA," and enriched by a preface from the master-printer's pen.

Beside having the usual four-leaf end-papers, it starts with a blank leaf and the following short title with a blank verso:—

(139)

UTOPIA WRITTEN BY SIR THOMAS MORE.

The "Foreword by William Morris" fills pages iii to viii; and a reprint of Raphe Robynson's title follows with a blank

verso ; his preface occupies pages xi to xiv, and the book occupies pages 1 to 282.   The colophon, with a blank verso, is—

> Now revised by F. S. Ellis & printed again/ by William
> Morris at the Kelmscott Press,/ Hammersmith, in the
> County of Middle-/ sex.   Finished the 4th day of August,
> 1893.
>   [the lesser bookmark]
> Sold by Reeves & Turner, 196, Strand.

A week later Morris had paid Tennyson the tribute of printing at the Press *Maud, a Monodrama ;* and he had almost
completed the quarto *Sidonia the Sorceress,* the prospectus of
which, issued from the Press, ranks as a work by him, though
            it is but two quarto leaves, without title,—first a
(140)   page about the book, signed William Morris, followed
            by a specimen page, an order form, and, on page 4,
the larger Kelmscott book-mark.   The book itself, translated
from Meinhold by the late Lady Wilde (" Speranza ") does not
fall to be here described.   In this year he contributed a Preface
to " Comrade " Steele's *Medieval Lore,* of which the title runs
thus :—

(141)

MEDIEVAL LORE :/ AN EPITOME OF/ *THE SCIENCE,
GEOGRAPHY, ANIMAL AND/ PLANT FOLK-LORE
AND MYTH OF/ THE MIDDLE AGE :/* BEING/ CLASSI-
FIED GLEANINGS FROM THE ENCYCLOPEDIA OF/ BARTHOLO-
MEW ANGLICUS/ ON THE PROPERTIES OF THINGS./ EDITED
BY/ ROBERT STEELE./ *WITH A PREFACE BY/* WILLIAM
MORRIS,/ AUTHOR OF 'THE EARTHLY PARADISE.'/ LONDON :/
ELLIOT STOCK, 62, PATERNOSTER ROW, E.C./
1893.

This is a handsome 8vo. of x + 156 pages, bound in bright
buff buckram lettered in brown.

   This year 1893 also saw the resurrection of *Socialism from
the Root Up* with a new title.   This remarkable work of true
collaboration, in which both Morris and Mr. Bax went over
every sentence, was now dug out of *The Commonweal,* revised,
and printed as

(142)

SOCIALISM

ITS GROWTH & OUTCOME

BY

WILLIAM MORRIS

AUTHOR OF 'THE EARTHLY PARADISE,' 'NEWS FROM NOWHERE,' ETC.

AND

E. BELFORT BAX

AUTHOR OF 'HISTORY OF PHILOSOPHY,' 'THE RELIGION OF
SOCIALISM,' ETC.

LONDON
SWAN SONNENSCHEIN & Co.
NEW YORK: CHARLES SCRIBNER'S SONS
1893

This is a crown 8vo. of viii + 335 pages nicely printed, with
paging in the outer corners, head-lines, "SOCIALISM" on
versos, and according to the sectional subject on rectos, and the
imprint at the foot of page 335 "*Printed by* R. & R. CLARK,
Edinburgh." The large-paper copies are "called an edition,"
and rightly; they are 275 in number, demy 8vo. on
(143) hand-made paper, bound in red buckram, and labelled
"SOCIALISM/ ITS GROWTH/ AND OUTCOME/
WILLIAM MORRIS/ E. BELFORT BAX."
A two-page 8vo. leaflet belongs to this time,—a letter
to the Editor of *The Daily Chronicle* dated the 9th of November
and printed on the 10th. The leaflet is headed

(144)

HELP FOR THE MINERS.

Daily Chronicle, Nov. 10TH, 1893.

THE DEEPER MEANING OF THE STRUGGLE.

The imprint at the end of page 2 is "BAINES & SCARSBROOK,
PRINTERS, 75, FAIRFAX ROAD, SOUTH HAMPSTEAD."

The third volume of the Saga Library was issued in 1893 :—

(145)

THE STORIES OF THE KINGS OF NORWAY CALLED THE ROUND WORLD

(HEIMSKRINGLA)

BY SNORRI STURLUSON

DONE INTO ENGLISH
OUT OF THE ICELANDIC.

BY

WILLIAM MORRIS

AND

EIRÍKR MAGNÚSSON.

VOL. I [II, III, IV]

WITH A LARGE MAP OF NORWAY

LONDON
BERNARD QUARITCH, 15 PICCADILLY
1893

Of this book, which is to be in four volumes, Vol. I. consists of viii + 410 pages, Vol. II. of viii + 484 pages, and Vol. III. (1895) of viii + 505 pages.   Vol. IV. is not yet out.   The words " with a large map of Norway " only appear on the title of Vol. I.

In this busy year the fourth Autumn exhibition of the Arts and Crafts Society was held (the third had been in 1890).   In the catalogue is a delightful little poem by Morris for some bed-hangings at Kelmscott Manor.   He also lectured for the Society on the printing of books, and allowed a hand-press of his to be set up in the centre hall, where people were shown Kelmscott printing practically.   There and then the lecture on Gothic Architecture which he had delivered for the Society in 1889 was printed as a 16mo. volume in the golden type in black and red and sold for half a crown.   The title is—

(146)

GOTHIC ARCHITECTURE:
A LECTURE FOR THE ARTS
AND CRAFTS EXHIBITION
SOCIETY [leaf] BY WILLIAM
MORRIS.

This is on a single leaf with blank verso; and there are 68 pages of text, with the colophon—

> This paper, first spoken as a lec-/ ture at the New Gallery, for the/ Arts and Crafts Exhibition Society,/ in the year 1889, was printed by the/ Kelmscott Press during the Arts/ and Crafts Exhibition at the New/ Gallery, Regent Street, London,/ 1893/ Sold by William Morris, Kelms-/ cott Press, Upper Mall, Hammer-/ smith.

The book was done up in blue-grey and in Turner-grey boards, with linen backs, and the title printed on the front cover. There were three editions, each of 500 copies, in the second of which some errors were corrected. In the first
(147-8) Van Eyck's name is spelt *Van Eyk* at the top of page 45. There were 45 copies printed on vellum. The lectures on Textiles, on Dyeing, and on Printing, with Essays by other members of the Society, were now gathered into a volume with the following title :—

(149)

Arts And Crafts Essays

BY

Members of the Arts and Crafts
Exhibition Society

With A Preface
By William Morris

London
RIVINGTON, PERCIVAL, & CO.
1893

This book is a crown 8vo. of xviii + 420 pages, printed by Clark, with a 32-page catalogue inserted, bound in dark red buckram and labelled " ARTS & CRAFTS/ ESSAYS/ PREFACE BY/ *William Morris.*"

In October a volume containing Rossetti's *Ballads and Narrative Poems* was finished at the Kelmscott Press, where Morris closed his year's out-put with his own translation of *King Florus.* This, though uniform in size and binding with the *Gothic Architecture*, is more decorative. It is in the Chaucer type, in black and red, and has a designed title-page and first-page border. The half-title, which gives the true name of the book, is—

(150)

THE TALE OF KING FLORUS
AND THE FAIR JEHANE.

This has a blank verso; and on the verso of the next leaf is the engraved title which faces this page. There are 96 pages of text, and a leaf with the recto colophon—

Printed by William Morris/ at the Kelmscott Press, Upper/ Mall, Hammersmith, in the/ County of Middlesex, & fin-/ ished on the 16th day of De-/ cember, 1893./ Sold by William Morris at the/ Kelmscott Press.

The true title is reproduced on the front cover. Before the next volume of this series was out—for it is a series of three—the illustrated *Glittering Plain* already described, Rossetti's Sonnets and Lyrical Poems, and Keats's Poems, had passed through the Press. Then came

(151)

OF THE FRIENDSHIP
OF AMIS AND AMILE.

Uniform with *King Florus*, it has the same borders to the frontispiece or title-page (worded precisely as the above half-title is) and the first page. Besides these two leaves, there are 65 pages of the tale, and two leaves on the first of which (recto) the colophon is printed (all but the last two lines in red)—

OF KING FLORUS and the FAIR JEHANE

VERSO TITLE-PAGE OR FRONTISPIECE DESIGNED BY MORRIS.

Here ends the Story of Amis/ & Amile, done out of the an-/ cient French into English, by/ William Morris, and printed/ by the said William Morris/ at the Kelmscott Press, 14,/ Upper Mall, Hammersmith,/ in the County of Middlesex ;/ finished on the 13th day of/ March, of the year 1894./ Sold by William Morris, at/ the Kelmscott Press.

The Story of Amis and Amile has been reprinted separately in the United States and included in Mr. Mosher's quaint little series known as " the Brocade Series." The title-page, of which the first and last lines are in red, is

(152)

THE STORY OF AMIS & AMILE/ DONE OUT OF THE ANCIENT/ FRENCH INTO ENGLISH BY/ WILLIAM MORRIS/ [BOOK-MARK] PORTLAND MAINE/ THOMAS B MOSHER/ MDCCCXCVI.

There is a half-title, " THE STORY OF/ AMIS & AMILE," with note on the verso as to the two previous issues, two pages of " Foreword," half-title repeated, pages 9 to 47 of text, and on page 48 the colophon in even small capitals (*very* small) " Four hundred and twen-/ ty-five copies of this/ book have been printed/ on Japan vellum, and/ type distributed, in the/ month of August, a.d./ mdcccxcvi, at the press/ of George D. Loring,/ Portland, Maine." " Japanese vellum " is the usual trade mis-description of fine smooth Japanese paper. There is a wrapper of the same, with the title printed in capitals imitated from those of Morris's golden type, and a brown ornamental capital T badly imitated from one of his. The tiny volume has a slip case of card-board covered with a paper imitation of brocade : its two companions in this misery of transatlantic fussiness, *The Child in the House* and *A Pageant of Summer*, are similarly treated ; and the three volumes are enclosed in a box covered with the same paper.

Before Morris completed his series of three little volumes from the French, he had finished printing *Atalanta in Calydon* and his own *Wood beyond the World ;* but it is best to finish first describing the set of French tales of which the next and last is—

(153)

THE TALE OF THE
EMPEROR COUSTANS
AND OF OVER SEA.

Before the above half-title there are two blank leaves, and after it the ornamental title or frontispiece (verso) with the legend " THE TALE/ OF KING/ COUS-/ TANS EM/ PEROR OF/ BYZANCE." There are 38 pages of the tale, and a colophon in red with a black capital

> HERE withal endeth the/ Story of King Coustans/ the Emperor./ The said story was done/ out of the ancient French into/ English by William Morris.

Page 39 is a half-title, "THE HISTORY OF OVER/ SEA," on the verso of which is an ornamental title, " A TALE/ OF/ OVER/ SEA": that tale extends from page 41 to page 130, where the colophon, red all but the capital and the last two lines, reads as follows :—

> HERE ends the Story of/ Over Sea, done out of/ ancient French into Eng-/lish by William Morris./ This book, the Stories of the/ Emperor Coustans, and of/ Over Sea, was printed by Wil-/ liam Morris at the Kelmscott/ Press, Upper Mall, Hammer-/smith, in the County of Mid-/ lesex, & finished on the 30th/ day of August, 1894./ Sold by William Morris at the/ Kelmscott Press.

The contents of these three little books were republished in a single crown 8vo. volume by Mr. Allen, having on the verso of the half-title ("OLD FRENCH/ ROMANCES") Mr. Crane's design—the St. George and Dragon executed for Mr. Allen with his mono-gram. Of this book, printed at the Ballantyne Press in London, the title-page is—

(154)

OLD FRENCH/ ROMANCES/ DONE INTO ENGLISH/
BY/ WILLIAM MORRIS/ WITH AN INTRODUCTION
BY/ JOSEPH JACOBS/ LONDON/ GEORGE ALLEN,
RUSKIN HOUSE/ 1896/ *All rights reserved*

For the rest the book consists of xxxii + 169 pages, bound in
plain red cloth and gilt-lettered at the back " OLD/ FRENCH/
ROMANCES/ W. MORRIS/ GEORGE ALLEN."

It was from his own press again that his next romance was
first issued—

(155)

THE WOOD BEYOND THE WORLD.
BY WILLIAM MORRIS.

These two lines, at the top of the recto of the third leaf in a
sheet, are all the title the book has. The next leaf is a
delightful frontispiece by Sir Edward Burne-Jones, with a
blank recto, and completes signature a. Signature b starts
with the opening of Chapter I. within a border like that of the
frontispiece, and with an ornamental A two inches square.
There are 260 pages printed in the Chaucer type, and subjected
in red at the top of the outer margins. The chapters are also
headed in red. There is an abundance of ornamental capitals
both small and medium-sized, and also of beautiful marginal
ornaments. The colophon gives the information usual in a
title-page :—

> HERE ends the tale of the Wood beyond/ the World,
> made by William Morris, and/ printed by him at the
> Kelmscott Press,/ Upper Mall, Hammersmith. Finished
> the/ 30th day of May, 1894.
> [smaller book-mark]
> Sold by William Morris, at the Kelmscott/ Press.

This is on the recto of the third leaf in signature s, paged 261 ;
the verso is blank ; and a blank leaf completes the sheet. The
binding is of vellum with silk ties ; and the end-papers consist
of complete sheets—four leaves instead of two as usual—one
being the paste-down at each end. The paper is trimmed,

12

both at the foot and at the fore-edge. The binding is lettered
in gold on a flat back, "THE WOOD/ BEYOND/ THE
WORLD/ BY/ WILLIAM/ MORRIS." The issue consisted
of 350 copies on paper and eight on vellum. Although the
printing was finished in May, the book was not actually issued
to the subscribers till the 16th of October 1894.

Soon after the Kelmscott edition, another issue of *The Wood
beyond the World* was published in the ordinary way, with the
following title-page :—

(156)

THE WOOD BEYOND THE/ WORLD. BY WILLIAM/
    MORRIS./ [book-mark]/ LONDON: LAWRENCE
    AND BULLEN,/ 16, HENRIETTA STREET, COVENT/
    GARDEN. MDCCCXCV.

THE LAWRENCE AND BULLEN BOOK-
MARK DESIGNED BY WALTER CRANE.

The *format* of the volume is that
described as square crown 8vo.
The paper appears to be an imperial cut in halves and worked as
an 8vo. ; but every sheet really
yields 16 leaves, as may be seen
from the alternation of the sham
deckel edges and cut edges at foot.
A preliminary half-sheet (8vo.) consists of a blank leaf with the signature A on the recto, a half-title
("THE WOOD BEYOND THE
WORLD.") with blank verso, the title with imprint at the
foot of the verso, reading "CHISWICK PRESS:— CHARLES
WHITTINGHAM AND CO./ TOOKS COURT, CHANCERY LANE,
LONDON." and two pages of "Contents" numbered v and
vi. The text consists of 250 boldly printed pages without
head-lines or shoulder-notes, centrally numbered in Arabic
figures at foot, and followed by a leaf bearing on the centre of
the recto a repetition of the imprint, but under a Chiswick
Press lion, dolphin, and anchor. The chapters are com-
menced on fresh pages, with dropped heads, the number of
each chapter and the subject being given in bold Roman
capitals. Thus the book is in a manner a compromise between
the Kelmscott style and the conventional style current at the

present day. The binding is of plain dark red buckram with white end-papers, gilt-lettered at the back "THE WOOD/ BEYOND/ THE WORLD/ WILLIAM/ MORRIS/ LAW-RENCE/ & BULLEN." Fifty copies were printed on What-man's hand-made paper of practically the same size, and produced in the same way by cutting the sheet in two and working it as an 8vo. The hand-made sheets when folded knock up so as to leave the foot a little less even than the machine-made sheets do, and so require slightly larger covers. These are of lichen-coloured "art linen," unblocked, with white end-papers, and back-labels printed in a similar colour, and reading thus :— " The Wood/ beyond/ the World/ William Morris." The first leaf has the following certificate on the verso :—" *Fifty copies printed on Whatman's Paper./ No.* "; and each copy is numbered in manuscript. The words " The Wood beyond the World," " Lawrence and Bullen," and " MDCCCXCV" are printed in red in the Whatman copies. Two spare back-labels printed on one slip, side by side, follow the last leaf ; and a third is on the otherwise plain drab paper wrapper in which each of these choice volumes was delivered.

Socialism and " Sagaism " are both represented in this year 1894,—" Sagaism " by Vol. II. of the *Heimskringla* (already described), and Socialism by a choice little private print :—

(157)

LETTERS
ON SOCIALISM,

BY

William Morris.

London : *Privately Printed.*
1894.

As denoted by the book-mark on page 31, this book belongs to the Ashley Library of Mr. Thomas J. Wise. It has a half-title " LETTERS ON SOCIALISM," the title, a certificate

12—2

that only 34 copies were printed, a note with blank verso, a half-title, " LETTERS," and pages 3 to 30 of text. It is bound in Japanese paper boards gilt-lettered up the back " LETTERS ON SOCIALISM — WILLIAM MORRIS — 1894." A four-page letter is given in facsimile as frontispiece. Of the 34 copies 4 were printed on fine writing vellum. Very different in style is the next piece. Morris had contributed to a paper called *Liberty*, in February 1894, an article—*Why I am a Communist*. This was reprinted in a demy 8vo. pamphlet of 16 pages without wrapper, but with a title-page in which Mr. Crane's League design was adapted without his knowledge :—

(158)

SECOND SERIES

LIBERTY PRESS

The Why I Ams.

WHY I AM A COMMUNIST,
By WILLIAM MORRIS.

WHY I AM AN EXPROPRIATIONIST,
By L. S. BEVINGTON.

LONDON :
PRINTED AND PUBLISHED BY JAMES TOCHATTI,
" LIBERTY " PRESS.
1894.

PRICE ONE PENNY.

In September 1894 Morris wrote a Preface for a pretty book of wood-cuts with the following title, drawn in ornamental letters :—

(159)

GOOD KING/ WENCESLAS/ A CAROL WRITTEN
BY DR. NEALE AND/ PICTURED BY ARTHUR
J. GASKIN WITH/ AN INTRODUCTION BY
WILLIAM MORRIS./ BIRMINGHAM. MESSRS.
CORNISH BRS./ NEW STREET MDCCCXCV.

It is a quarto, consisting of 12 leaves,—the first blank on
both sides, and the rest blank on one side. Besides a half-title,
title, dedication, note, and preface, there are six full-page
wood-cuts. The book is bound in blue paper boards with a
wood-cut on the front cover, and has end-papers of four leaves
each including paste-downs.

Morris's next work is one of translation *The Tale of Beowulf;*
but before it was issued he had put forth from his press Mr.
Wardrop's translation of *The Book of Wisdom and Lies,*
Psalmi Penitentiales, Epistola de Contemptu Mundi, and the
first volume of Shelley's Poems. The *Beowulf* is a quarto with
a very fine designed title, bound in limp vellum with three silk
ties, gilt-lettered " BEOWULF" up the back. It starts with a
blank leaf. The third page bears the single line " THE TALE
OF BEOWULF." Pages iv to vi are the argument; the
recto title comes on page viii; and the lettering within the
sumptuous border reads, in white upon a black flowered
ground,

(160)

the tale of
Beowulf
sometime
king of the
folk of the
Weder
Geats

The text begins at page 1 within a counterpart border and
extends to page 110, is very nobly ornamented in numerous

margins, and has shoulder-notes etc. in red.   The colophon on page 111 is

> Here endeth the Story of Beowulf, done out of the Old/ English tongue by William Morris & A. J. Wyatt, and/ printed by the said William Morris at the Kelmscott/ Press, Upper Mall, Hammersmith, in the County of/ Middlesex, and finished on the 10th day of January/ 1895   [the larger book-mark]
> Sold by William Morris at the Kelmscott Press.

The colophon is followed by pages 112 to 119 containing an index and glossary in the Chaucer type.

Before his next romance he printed *Syr Percyvelle of Gales,* the second volume of Shelley's Poems, and the quarto *Jason* already described.

In the summer of 1895 he issued from his press a delightful prose romance which he had originally begun to write in four-foot trochaic couplets, but had desisted before completing the seventeenth line.   The proper title of this book is

(161)

CHILD CHRISTOPHER AND
GOLDILIND THE FAIR. BY
WILLIAM MORRIS. [VOL. II.]

This book is in two volumes printed in black and red in the Chaucer type, and is uniform in size etc. with the romances from the French.   Page 1 in each volume is as above.   Vol. I. has a verso ornamental title of which the lettering is " Of Child/ Christo-/ pher and/ fair Gold-/ ilind "—and 256 pages of text with an erratum-slip inserted.   Vol. II. has 238 pages of text, and, on page 239, the colophon, printed in red except the last two lines,—

> Here ends the Story of/ Child Christopher & Gold-/ ilind the Fair ; made by Wil-/liam Morris, and printed by/ him at the Kelmscott Press,/ Upper Mall, Hammersmith,/ in the County of Middlesex/ Finished the 25th day of/ July, 1895./   Sold by William Morris at/ the Kelmscott Press.

These volumes have, on their linen backs, printed labels reading
" CHILD/ CHRISTO-/ PHER/ I [II]." The third volume
of Shelley issued from the Press in the course of August,
Rossetti's *Hand and Soul* in October, and Mr. Ellis's selection
from Herrick in November. It is to be mentioned here that,
in November 1894, a remarkable half-crown magazine called
The Quest had been started at Birmingham, printed at the
press of the Guild of Handicraft. It drew its inspiration
from the Kelmscott Press, and is a very sightly small 4to.
with bold wood-cuts. Six numbers were published; and to
the fourth (November 1895) Morris contributed an account of
Kelmscott Manor. Some separate copies of this were done
with the following title—

(162)

GOSSIP about an old
House on the Upper
Thames written by
WILLIAM MORRIS.

November, 1895.

This choice little book, of the same typography as the magazine,
consists of half-title, " GOSSIP ABOUT AN OLD HOUSE,"
title, verso wood-cut of Kelmscott Manor House as in *News
from Nowhere*, pages 5 to 14 of text including two more
Kelmscott wood-cuts (by Mr. New), and, on the recto of the
first of two leaves, the colophon—

> PRINTED AT THE PRESS OF THE BIRMING-
> HAM GUILD OF HANDICRAFT LIMITED,
> PUBLISHED IN "THE QUEST" FOR NOVEM-
> BER MDCCCXCV, AND FIFTY COPIES DONE IN
> THIS SEPARATE FORM.

The book is done up in mottled grey hand-made paper boards,
lettered on the front cover " GOSSIP ABOUT AN OLD
HOUSE." The end-papers, following the Kelmscott fashion,
are complete sheets of four leaves.

Mr. Ellis's selection from Coleridge's poems was finished at the Kelmscott Press on the 5th of February 1896; and the second of March saw the completion of *The Well at the World's End.* Of this largest of Morris's prose works two separate prints must be described under the head of *editiones principes.* There is no doubt that the intention all along was to issue *The Well at the World's End* first from the Kelmscott Press, as announced very soon after the Press was established. Nevertheless the book was actually set up at the Chiswick Press from the author's finished manuscript; and from the Whittingham sheets the Kelmscott printers set the types for the intended first edition. At head quarters changes took place in the scheme of decoration. At first there was to be a long series of illustrations by Mr. Arthur J. Gaskin. This scheme, however, was abandoned; and that of four designs by Sir Edward Burne-Jones took its place, and occupied considerable further time in the execution. Meanwhile, the Chiswick Press book, tasteful but more or less on the conventional lines adopted in the book trade, was completed in 1894 and was ready to follow hard upon the steps of the great Kelmscott double-column quarto. Both books were originally to have been published by Messrs. Reeves and Turner; and things went so far at Took's Court that the title-pages of the two 8vo. volumes were set up; the edition was actually complete; and a single copy was gathered from the stock and bound in the grey paper boards with linen backs by which we know the " outer book " as now issued by Messrs. Longman. This copy had no labels. Its title-pages read as follows:—

(163)

THE WELL AT THE
WORLD'S END A TALE
BY WILLIAM MORRIS

VOLUME I [II]

LONDON: REEVES AND TURNER
5, WELLINGTON STREET, STRAND
MDCCCXCIV

Well at World's End, first draft

William Morris

of his house which was new and goodly
sniffing the sweet scent of the morning he
was clad in a goodly long gown of grey
with silver neck for the summer tide - for little
he wrought with his hands and much
with his tongue he was a man of 60 summers
black bearded and ruddy and his name was
Clement Chapman When he saw Ralph he
smiled kindly, and came and held his stirrup
and said Welcome lord! art thou come to
eat and drink and give a message in a poor
pedlar's house. Yea said Ralph smiting (for
he was hungry: I will eat & drink with the
and go my way. And he got off his horse &
the Carle led him into his house And if it
were goodly without within it was better
For there was a fair chamber panelled
with carven work well wrought, and a cupboard
of no sorry state, and the chairs & stools
as fair as might be, no kings might be better
and the windows were glazed and there were
flowers & pears in them and
the bed was hung with goodly webs from
over sea such as the Soldan loveth also
whereas his ware bowers were hard by the chamber

REDUCED FAC-SIMILE: FROM HOLOGRAPH MANUSCRIPT OF "THE WELL
AT THE WORLD'S END."

Each of these 8vo. volumes has a half-title ("THE WELL AT THE WORLD'S END") and list of Contents (Chapter-headings). In Vol. I. the "Contents" occupies three pages (2 leaves), —in Vol. II., two pages (1 leaf). The text of Vol. I. is 378, that of Vol. II., 279. In Vol. I. there is a leaf after the text with the imprint (on the recto) " CHISWICK PRESS :— C. WHITTINGHAM AND CO.,/ TOOKS COURT, CHANCERY LANE." In Vol. II. the same imprint is on the verso of p. 279 with a small lion and anchor book-mark over it. The 8vo. volumes are without head-lines: they are paged at the foot in Arabic figures. The whole issue was printed on French hand-made paper; but the book described above, so far as its title-pages are concerned, is said to be unique, although there were once 1000 copies of it.

It was no later than the 14th of December 1893 that the two 8vo. volumes were through the press at Tooks Court; but not until the 2nd of March 1896, as we have seen, was the Kelmscott quarto wholly printed; and not until the 4th of June did it reach subscribers from Leighton's bindery. This noble quarto made a new departure. It was printed in the Chaucer type, two columns on a page, with four designs by Sir Edward Burne-Jones surrounded by Morris's own borders. These form frontispieces to the four books of the romance; and

within the border facing each of these frontispieces the chapter opens with a large ornamental word instead of capital. Of these words, that which begins the story, " Long," is here given. There is great wealth of marginal ornaments and larger and smaller capitals; and the chapter-headings are in red. On the third leaf of the book is the simple title—

(164)

THE WELL AT THE WORLDS END BY WILLIAM MORRIS.

The fourth leaf is the first verso frontispiece ; and the story extends to page 495, on which the right-hand column ends with the colophon—

HERE ends the Well at/ the World's End, writ-/ten by William Morris,/ with four pictures designed by/ Sir Edward Burne-Jones/ Printed by William Morris at/ the Kelmscott Press, 14, Up-/per Mall, Hammersmith, in the/ County of Middlesex, and fin-/ished on the 2nd day of March,/ 1896.

Across the page below both columns is printed in red " Sold by William Morris at the Kelmscott Press." On page 496, at the top, is the larger book-mark. The binding is of limp vellum with three silk ties and is gilt-lettered across the back " THE WELL/ AT THE/ WORLD'S END/ BY/ WILLIAM/ MORRIS." Another change was now necessary. Not only had Messrs. Reeves and Turner ceded the publication of this book ; but arrangements had been made with Messrs. Longman to be Morris's publishers. Hence, while *The Well at the World's End* in its more sumptuous form was sold from the Kelmscott Press, it was necessary to print fresh titles for the edition in two volumes which, according to the program, was to follow. This was in due time done ; and the title-pages of (165) the regularly published books have Messrs. Longmans' imprint. They are done up like No. 163, and labelled " MORRIS/ THE/ WELL/ AT THE/ WORLD'S/ END/ VOL. I. [II.]." Morris made one more anonymous contribution to the literature of the " Anti-scrape," namely—

(166)

THE SOCIETY FOR THE PROTECTION OF ANCIENT BUILDINGS.

ON THE EXTERNAL COVERINGS OF ROOFS.

This is a double leaflet, four pages, with no title-page or date, but headed as above, and with the address " 9 Buckingham

Street, Strand," printed at the foot of page 4. There are no head-lines or numerals. It is well printed on good, smooth, toned paper, and measures $8\frac{1}{16} \times 5\frac{5}{16}$ inches.

Three more books are to be mentioned as having issued from the Kelmscott Press in the poet's life-time beside the volumes of *The Earthly Paradise* already described, namely the renowned folio Chaucer, the quarto *Laudes Beatæ Mariæ Virginis*, and *The Floure and the Leafe* (a small quarto); and an 8vo. edition of Spenser's *Shepheardes Calender* with twelve beautiful wood-cuts after Mr. Gaskin, has appeared since Morris's death. As an example of the beauty of design lavished by the master-printer on the folio Chaucer, I give below one of the large intitial words, the old Chaucerian " Whan," which is also used to decorate the first page of *The Floure and the Leafe.*

Immediately after Morris's death Mr. H. M. Hyndman wrote a sympathetic account of him in *Justice.* This, together with an article and some paragraphs contributed by Morris to that paper for May Day 1895 and 1896, was reprinted at the

Twentieth Century Press as a sixteen-page pamphlet with a
portrait of Morris outside,—above it the words "HOW I
BECAME A SOCIALIST" and below it "WILLIAM
MORRIS/ Price One Penny." The ordinary issue has no
other title-page; but there are special copies with a stiff
green paper wrapper bearing the following title :

(167)

How I Became a Socialist.

BY

WILLIAM MORRIS.

*With some account of his connection with the
Social-Democratic Federation*

BY H. M. HYNDMAN.

LONDON: OCTOBER, 1896.

Since the Introduction to this book was in type, Morris's
trustees have issued from the Kelmscott Press

(168)

THE WATER OF THE WONDROUS ISLES
BY WILLIAM MORRIS.

This is the wording of the half-title on the recto of the fourth
leaf of signature a, the first three leaves being blank. The book
is a Kelmscott quarto, printed in the Chaucer type in double
columns with red shoulder-notes and chapter-headings. There
are 344 pages of text, followed by the larger book-mark, which
is on the recto of z3 over the words "Sold by the Trustees of
the late William Morris at the Kelmscott Press"; and z4 is
blank. The story is divided into seven parts. The first page
of each is surrounded by a border (not the first two pages
by a pair of borders); and six out of the seven parts have
initial words of the width of the column as in *The Well
at the World's End.* Part V. has no initial word—only an
ornamental letter an inch square. A great number of pages
are decorated with the well-known flower and leaf margin
ornaments of the Press. At the end of each part is a colo-

phon in the Troy type right across the page. The first reads thus

> Here ends the First Part of the Water of the Won-/drous Isles, which is called Of the House of Captiv-/ity. And now begins the Second Part, which is called/ Of the Wondrous Isles.

This quaint formula varies a little from book to book ; and the final colophon is

> Here ends The Water of the Wondrous Isles, written/ by William Morris. It was printed at the Kelmscott/ Press, Upper Mall, Hammersmith, in the County of/ Middlesex, & finished on the first day of April, 1897./ The borders and ornaments were designed entirely/ by William Morris, except the initial words Whilom/ & Empty, which were completed from his unfinished/ designs by R. Catterson-Smith.

It is to be added that the other words, save " So " at page 46, are, with the borders, repetitions from *The Well at the World's End.* The book is bound in limp vellum with three silk ties, gilt-lettered across the back "THE WATER/ OF THE/ WONDROUS/ ISLES./ BY/ WILLIAM/ MORRIS." Each end-paper is of four leaves counting the paste-down.

It is with regret that I send this work out uncompleted by the bibliographical details of the last of all Morris's romances, *The Sundering Flood*, which is still unpublished, and that, for the same reason, I am unable to describe either the edition of *Sigurd the Volsung* or the impression of *Love is Enough*, in black, red, and blue, promised by the author's trustees as the last works from the Kelmscott Press. Each one of these greater examples of his printing brings before me vividly not only the master-printer, but the consummate artist, and the true, strong, British man ; and I would gladly linger with him a while longer. Those who knew and loved William Morris —and to know him was to love him—may well be thinking still, though a year has passed since he died, that sixty-two years and a half are but a little span of life for a man of his native vigour and robust habit. They can scarcely yet take their stand on the platform whence the public view the matter

—the great public who have gained so much from the life cut short on the 3rd of October 1896—who knew not the man, but saw everywhere the output of his energy and genius, and who can but say, if the question of his "allotted span" occurs to them : "Morris? Well, he has published volumes and volumes of fine poetry, numbers of prose romances, translated epics and sagas from the Greek, the Latin, the Icelandic; poured forth polemical tracts and treatises ; carried on a fine-art decoration business which during some thirty years has been steadily revolutionizing British tastes in matters of building, decoration, and upholstery ; led for years that section of the Socialists whose demands are founded upon reason, editing several volumes of their journal ; and lastly set up and carried on a press from which have issued quite a number of books, forming, perhaps, the finest examples of printing ever seen."

Such a mass of work, to the public mind, must bring visions of a man "well stricken in years." But to those who were privileged to know him it was a standing wonder that Morris, at the age of sixty, and not looking sixty, had done all this work in the world—so various, so thorough, and so full of the most valuable qualities—and yet always found time to receive his friends and acquaintance, and give them the benefit not only of his hearty, cheery companionship, but also of his unerring judgment and vast learning in all matters connected with the ways and means of beautifying the world and man's life in the world. Last autumn, if England did but know it, William Morris was the living Englishman she could least afford to lose. His friends have to bear his loss with the rest of his countrymen ; but they have a far deeper loss. The personal qualities which made up the character of this man of genius would have been irresistibly attractive even if he had had no genius at all. Kindliness, sagacity, courage, good comradeship, an inveterate habit of acting upon convictions deliberately formed, and an unswerving sense of honour and true decorum are admirable personal traits to find in one man—apart from genius and erudition : he had them all ; and their combination is not so common that his friends can afford to remember and regret the genius more than the man.

APPENDIX.

Besides a few matters which are more proper to an appendix than to the body of a book like the present, there are some which had no existence till recently and some which have but lately come to my knowledge, or which I have not till now been able to verify positively. Among the last is the reprint of *Gunnlaug's Saga* in the Caxton type of the Chiswick Press, of which I saw some pages in the Arts and Crafts Exhibition of 1890; but they were merely described (p. 248 of the catalogue) as a specimen of the fount of type; and I could not at the time follow up the question whether they represented a book. They did represent a privately printed pot quarto of eight sheets, 75 copies on paper (hand-made), and three on fine vellum. They were intended for decoration by means of illuminated initials &c.; and spaces for large capitals were left.

Mr. Mosher of Portland, Maine, has made a sort of piratical first edition which it seems necessary to catalogue—namely *The Hollow Land*. I do not refer to the mere transfer of that early story of Morris's from *The Oxford and Cambridge Magazine* to *The Bibelot, a Reprint of Poetry and Prose chosen in part from Scarce Editions and Sources not generally known;* for besides reprinting the tale in his magazine, Mr. Mosher has issued it in the form of an independent book,—a form which it now takes for the first time. The title-page, of which the first and last lines are in red, runs thus :—

THE HOLLOW LAND
A TALE BY WILLIAM
MORRIS

[book-mark]

Portland, Maine
THOMAS B. MOSHER
Mdcccxcvij

13

This 16mo. volume starts with 4 blank-verso'd leaves, namely
a half-title, "THE HOLLOW LAND," a certificate,
the title, and a sonnet signed "Francis Sherman." Then
come a 2-page preface, a second half-title like the first,
pages 5 to 78 of text, a blank leaf, a half-title, "NOTE," a
2-page note about *The Oxford and Cambridge Magazine*, and
two blank leaves. The head-lines ("THE HOLLOW LAND") are
of the hideous lop-sided kind now unhappily becoming fashion-
able, set against the back margin. The paging is at the foot
in Arabic figures. The book is printed on Japanese paper with
a wrapper of the same on the recto of which the three lines of
title are repeated, the words "THE HOLLOW LAND" being
printed up the back. The certificate reads thus :—" *Twenty-
five copies of this book/ printed on Japanese vellum, of/ which
twenty copies only are for sale./ This is No.* " [number filled
in in manuscript]. It is a treasurable little book enough; but
Morris objected to the revival of these immature stories; and
he was right.

Early in 1879 Morris began work seriously upon an attempt
" to make England independent of the East for the supply of
hand-made Carpets which may claim to be considered works of
art." A circular headed " The Hammersmith Carpets " and
dated " May 24th, 1880," was issued by the firm to its clients;
and that circular I have mentioned at page 98 as having
doubtless been written by the poet. Had I been in possession
of external evidence to support internal, I should have given
this quarto half-sheet (two leaves) of bluish hand-made paper,
bearing one page of print, its proper place among the books,
pamphlets, sheets, &c. It is an excellent little essay on its
subject. The firm reïssued it in the same form in October 1882;
and, in a pamphlet published by Messrs. Roberts Brothers of
Boston, Mass., in 1883, the text is printed with trifling alteration, and attributed to Morris. The firm has issued first and
last but few circulars about its undertakings; but two others
which preceded the pamphlet show marks of the poet's hand.
One is a succinct account of the twelve departments of art-
work which they undertake; and the other relates to their
" furniture prints " (hand-printed cotton, linen, and worsted
cloths). These circulars are practically embodied in the
American pamphlet, which is a hand-book to an exhibit of
fine-art furnishing material at the Boston Foreign Fair of

1883-4. This hand-book, full of learning, information, and good advice, on the subject of house decoration and furnishing, is a large 8vo. pamphlet, the precise size of which is indiscoverable, as the top, bottom, and fore-edge are trimmed. It appears to consist of two sheets placed one inside the other : these are stitched through the centre fold into a mottled grey wrapper. The title page is worded thus :—

THE

MORRIS EXHIBIT

AT

THE FOREIGN FAIR,

BOSTON, 1883-84.

—◦○✕○◦—

BOSTON :

ROBERTS BROTHERS.

1883.

On the verso is the imprint " 𝕮𝖆𝖒𝖇𝖗𝖎𝖉𝖌𝖊 :/ PRINTED BY JOHN WILSON AND SON,/ UNIVERSITY PRESS." Page 3 is blank, being the recto of a frontispiece, " Plan of Morris and Company's Space, Franklin Hall, Foreign Exhibition, Boston." The text fills pages 5 to 30 ; page 31 bears an advertizement relating to American Agents of the firm ; and page 32 is blank. Page 1 of the wrapper bears the inscription " 𝕿𝖍𝖊/ 𝕸𝖔𝖗𝖗𝖎𝖘 𝕰𝖝𝖍𝖎𝖇𝖎𝖙/ 𝕬𝖙/ 𝕿𝖍𝖊 𝕱𝖔𝖗𝖊𝖎𝖌𝖓 𝕱𝖆𝖎𝖗./ BOSTON, 1883." Page 3 is taken up by advertizements of the Boston editions of Morris's books : pages 2 and 4 are blank. The " Hammersmith Carpets " circular occurs at pages 9 and 10 of this pamphlet, introduced by the words " This is what Mr. Morris said about them in the circular announcing the beginning of this new manufacture in England." Not to rest on that alone, I have enquired about the authorship at 449 Oxford Street : there I was fortunate enough to meet Mr. Frank Smith, who has been with the firm some twenty-seven years, and who saw Morris write it. The poet's prose works are not complete without that little dissertation ; but, apart from that, the " Exhibit " pamphlet is valuable, and contains much that is indirectly his. It was actually written by Mr. Wardle, who was at Boston in charge of the show.

Morris's contributions to *The Commonweal* are of great importance; but, as those to *Justice* in its first year (see page 107) precede the others chronologically, it will be better to give the whole list of *Justice* poems and articles first. They are all signed "William Morris."

CONTRIBUTIONS TO "JUSTICE."

No. of Paper.	Page.	No. of Columns.	
1	2	$\frac{3}{4}$	"An Old Fable Retold."
,,	4	2	"The Principles of Justice." (With H. M. Hyndman & J. Taylor.)
4	2	1	"Order and Anarchy."
,,	4	$1\frac{3}{4}$	"The Bondholder's Battue." (With H. M. Hyndman.)
7	4	$1\frac{3}{4}$	"The Way Out. An Appeal to Genuine Radicals."
9	2	$1\frac{1}{4}$	"Art or No Art? Who shall settle it?"
12	5	$\frac{5}{8}$	"Chants for Socialists.—No. 2. The Voice of Toil."
13	2	$1\frac{1}{4}$	"Why Not?"
14	5	—	"Chants for Socialists.—No. 3. All for the Cause." Whole page.
15	4	$1\frac{3}{4}$	"The Dull Level of Life."
18	2	$1\frac{1}{2}$	"A Factory as it Might Be."
,,	5	$\frac{1}{4}$	"The Propaganda Fund."
19	4	$1\frac{1}{5}$	"Individualism at the Royal Academy."
20	2	$1\frac{1}{8}$	"Work in a Factory as it Might Be. II."
21	5	$\frac{1}{2}$	"Chants for Socialists.—No. 4. No Master."
24	2	$1\frac{1}{2}$	"Work in a Factory as it Might Be. III."
25	5	$\frac{1}{2}$	"The Propaganda Fund."
26	4	$1\frac{1}{3}$	"To Genuine Radicals."
27	4	2	"The Housing of the Poor."
28	5	$\frac{1}{3}$	"Propaganda Fund."
29	5	$\frac{3}{4}$	"Propaganda Fund."
30	4	$1\frac{1}{2}$	"Socialism in England in 1884."
34	4	$1\frac{1}{4}$	"Uncrowned Kings."
,,	5	—	"The Social Democratic Federation to the Trades Unions of Great Britain. September, 1884." Whole page. Signed with others.
36	3	$\frac{3}{4}$	"The Hammersmith Costermongers."
39	4	$1\frac{1}{4}$	"An Appeal to the Just."
,,	6	$\frac{1}{8}$	"Literary Courtesy."
44	2	$1\frac{3}{4}$	"The Lord Mayor's Show."

No. of Paper.	Page.	No. of Columns.	
46	4	1	" The Hackney Election."
49	2	1½	" Philanthropists."
433	1	2	" May-Day." [ten stanzas.]
538	1	½	" May-Day, 1894." [nine stanzas.]
544	6	1¾	" How I became a Socialist."
634	8	⅕	" Socialism and Art."
642	5	1½	" The Promise of May."

The Commonweal, an eight-page news-sheet, might be inaccurately described as a folio ; but, as it is folded at the top and has to be cut open, it is not a folio though of the folio shape. The size of the page averages about 14¾ by 10 inches.   The paper was paged for binding in yearly volumes, and was so bound and issued after the close of each year—at all events so far as regards the six volumes with which we are concerned. For the first volume a title-page and index were printed.   The title reads thus :—

THE

C O M M O N W E A L

(ORGAN OF THE SOCIALIST LEAGUE).

EDITED UNDER THE DIRECTION OF THE GENERAL COUNCIL

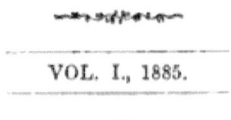

VOL. I., 1885.

London :

SOCIALIST LEAGUE OFFICE,

13, FARRINGDON ROAD, LONDON, E.C.

The verso is blank.   So is that of the " Index," which is more strictly speaking an alphabetically arranged table of contents

—three columns occupying one page. For the other volumes it was considered that no title-page and index could be afforded; and the only titles to be had were those for Vol. I., of which spare copies existed and could be got adapted, as I got them for my set. The volumes were bound in a sightly manner by Messrs. Burn in scarlet morocco-grained cloth, un-lettered at the back, but boldly lettered on the recto cover in black, "THE/ COMMONWEAL/ ·VOL· I· 1885" [and so on] with eight thin rules within a single thick one right across the top and bottom, in black on the recto and "blind" on the verso cover.

Volume I. contains eleven monthly numbers, February to December; and from April to September supplements of four pages were issued with the sheet. There are thus 112 pages; but the last page is numbered 108, the numerals 85-8 having been repeated on what should be pages 89-92.

Volume II. contains four monthly numbers and thirty-five weekly, beginning with that of the 1st of May, which has by way of supplement Mr. Crane's full-page cartoon, "Mrs. Grundy frightened at her own Shadow." There are thus 312 pages besides the picture, which is sometimes used as a frontis-piece to the volume.

Volume III. consists of fifty-three weekly numbers, 51 to 103, the year 1887 having begun and ended on a Saturday; and there are thus 424 pages.

Volumes IV. and V. consist of fifty-two numbers, 416 pages, each. With No. 166 (Vol. V., facing page 84) is Mr. Crane's cartoon "Vive la Commune," printed on the ordinary paper of the publication. It had been separately published a year earlier and was advertized in March and April 1888 in *The Commonweal*, as a picture for framing, printed on fine paper, price 2d. A reduction from it, 3×2 inches, appears in the advertizing columns of the paper for the 7th and 14th of April —similar to that used in the title-pages of some recent reprints of Morris's socialist pamphlets.

Volume VI. consists of forty-nine numbers, 392 pages. The paper remained a weekly till the end of November 1890. Morris's farewell contribution was an article headed "Where are we Now?" It appeared in the number for the 15th of November. In it the work of the socialist revival for the seven years during which Morris had been in the midst of it is summed up, the situation at the close of those years is described, the mode of action for the future inculcated, and, in an unpolemical way, the causes of the disruption pretty clearly indicated. In the next two numbers the new management appeal for funds, "copy," premises. Whether Morris gave them the "plant" I cannot say : it seems, at all events, that he was not going to pay the rent for a paper no longer to be carried on as he approved. But, whatever other "plant" they got, they had not only Mr. Crane's Freedom, Equality, Fraternity block, but also the big willow pattern block by Morris, which appeared on the first number of the new monthly series, with the startling sub-title

A JOURNAL OF

Revolutionary Socialism.

At this point *The Commonweal* passes beyond our ken. It struggled on in a way for a time and maintained a precarious existence until a question of incitement to murder arose, and the "plant" and stock as well as some of the people were seized by the police. All that there is further to say of this sixth volume of Morris's *Commonweal* concerns a few illustrations. In the number for the 1st of February 1890 is a hideous picture called "When will he get there ?" It represents a working man running up a winding road at the top of which is a wheat-sheaf, "the fruits of labour"; he has to pass an armed capitalist, landlord, policeman, and soldier. The same atrocity is the frontispiece to Morris's *Monopoly ;* and a reduction of it appears over and over again in the advertizing columns. In the number for the 29th of March is a still viler caricature of Mr. H. M. Stanley—"The Christian Pioneer." On the first page of the number for the 24th of May is Mr. Crane's beautiful and dignified "Labour's May Day" set in the midst of a chapter of *News from Nowhere* describing "how the change came." This is the design of which a reduced copy forms the frontispiece of the *editio princeps* of Morris's "Utopian Romance" (see page 147). A clever but ugly satirical design of "Capital and Labour," printed separately and given with the same number of the paper, completes the list of illustrations.

In the following list of Morris's contributions, it is to be understood that every item is signed in full, "William Morris," unless some other form of signature is specified. Each instalment of *Socialism from the Root Up* is signed "E. Belfort Bax and William Morris."

CONTRIBUTIONS TO "THE COMMONWEAL."

Vol. I.

No. of Paper.	Page.	No. of Columns.	
1	1	1	"Introductory."
,,	1	$2\frac{1}{2}$	"The Manifesto of the Socialist League."—William Morris and the Rest of the Provisional Council of the League.
,,	4	1	"The March of the Workers."
2	12	—	Unheaded Appeal for Subscriptions. 15 lines.
,,	12	1	"The Message of the March Wind."—[Section I. of "The Pilgrims of Hope."]
3	18	$1\frac{1}{2}$	"The Worker's Share of Art."
,,	20	$1\frac{1}{7}$	"The Pilgrims of Hope. II.—The Bridge and the Street."
,,	22	$\frac{1}{5}$	"Signs of the Times."—W. M.
4	32	$1\frac{1}{2}$	"The Pilgrims of Hope. III.—Sending to the War."
,,	35	$\frac{1}{6}$	"Signs of the Times."—W. M.
,,	36	$\frac{1}{2}$	"Monthly Report."—W. M.
,,	37	$1\frac{5}{6}$	"Unattractive Labour."
5	44	$1\frac{4}{5}$	"The Pilgrims of Hope. IV.—Mother and Son."
,,	49	$2\frac{1}{5}$	"Attractive Labour."
,,	52	$\frac{1}{5}$	Two Unheaded Paragraphs.—W. M.
6	53	2	"Notes on the Political Crisis."
,,	56	1	"Socialists at Play."
,,	61	$1\frac{1}{3}$	"Socialism and Politics. (An Answer to 'Another View.')"
7	65	$\frac{1}{2}$	"First General Meeting of the Socialist League."—William Morris. Edward B. Aveling.
,,	68	$1\frac{3}{5}$	"The Pilgrims of Hope. V.—New Birth."
,,	72	—	"Signs of the Times."—W. M. 8 lines.
8	77	$\frac{5}{6}$	"Mr. Chamberlain at Hull."
,,	80	$2\frac{1}{5}$	"The Pilgrims of Hope. VI.—The New Proletarian."

Vol. V.

14

No. of Paper.	Page.	No. of Columns.	
186	241	$1\frac{4}{7}$	"Notes on News."—W. M.
"	242	$1\frac{2}{3}$	"Impressions of the Paris Congress."—Concluded.
188	257	2	"Trial by Judge *v.* Trial by Jury."
"	261	$1\frac{1}{4}$	"Communism and Anarchism."
189	265	$\frac{7}{8}$	"Notes on News."—W. M.
191	281	$2\frac{1}{2}$	"The Lesson of the Hour."—W. M.
192	289	$1\frac{2}{3}$	"Notes on News."—W. M.
193	297	$\frac{7}{8}$	"Notes on News."—W. M.
194	305	$1\frac{3}{4}$	"Notes on News."—W. M.
197	329	$1\frac{1}{2}$	"Notes on News."—W. M.
198	337	$\frac{5}{8}$	"Notes on News."—W. M.
200	356	$\frac{3}{4}$	"Notes on News."—W. M.
201	361	$\frac{2}{3}$	"Notes on News."—W. M.
202	369	$1\frac{4}{5}$	"Notes on News."—W. M.
"	371	$\frac{1}{3}$	"A Death Song" (Reprinted).
203	377	1	"Notes on News."—W. M.
204	385	1	"Notes on News."—W. M.
"	388	2	"Monopoly."
205	393	$1\frac{2}{3}$	"Notes on News."—W. M.
"	394	$1\frac{3}{4}$	"Monopoly."—Continued.
206	401	$2\frac{1}{3}$	"Monopoly."—Concluded.—W. M.
207	409	$1\frac{1}{4}$	"Notes on News."—W. M.

Vol. VI.

209	9	$2\frac{1}{3}$	"News from Nowhere: Or, An Epoch of Rest. Being some Chapters from a Utopian Romance. Chap. I.—Discussion and Bed. Chap. II.—A Morning Bath."
210	18	2	"News from Nowhere: Chap. II. (continued).—A Morning Bath."
211	25	$2\frac{3}{5}$	"News from Nowhere: Chap. III.—The Guest House and Breakfast Therein."
"	28	$2\frac{1}{4}$	"Fabian Essays in Socialism."
212	33	$\frac{3}{4}$	"Notes on News."—W. M.
"	34	2	"News from Nowhere: Chap. III. (continued).—The Guest House and Breakfast Therein. Chap. IV.—A Market by the Way."
213	41	$\frac{3}{4}$	"Notes on News."—W. M.
"	42	$2\frac{1}{2}$	"News from Nowhere: Chap. V.—Children on the Road."

CONTRIBUTIONS TO OTHER NEWSPAPERS, MAGAZINES, AND REVIEWS,

WITH REFERENCES TO THE PAGES OF THE PRESENT VOLUME AT WHICH SOME OF THEM ARE MENTIONED.

The Story of Frithiof the Bold, *Dark Blue* (magazine), ch. i-x, March 1871 ch. xi-xv, April 1871 (pp. 79-82).

The First Foray of Aristomenes (p. 85), *Athenæum*, 13 May 1876.

Letter on England and the Turks (p. 93), *Daily News*, 26 October 1876.

Letter on " Restoration," *Athenæum*, 7 April 1877.

Letter on Canterbury Cathedral, *Times*, 4 June 1877.

      Do.,   Do., 7 July 1877.

Letter on Destruction of City Churches, *Times*, 17 April 1878.

Letter on St. Alban's Abbey, *Times*, 2 August 1878.

Quatrain for four paintings by Burne-Jones, Blackburn's Grosvenor Notes, 1879.

Letter on English Translations from the Icelandic, *Athenæum*, 17 May 1879.

Letter on the Restoration of St. Mark's at Venice, *Times*, 28 November 1879.

Letter on the same subject, *Times*, 29 November 1879.

Letter on Ashburnham House, *Daily News*, 28 November 1881.

Letter on High Wycomb Grammar School, *Athenæum*, 10 December 1881.

Letter on Vandalism in Italy, *Times*, 12 April 1882.

Letter on Impending Famine in Iceland, *Daily News*, 8 Aug. 1882.

Letter on River Pollution in Putney, *Daily News*, 15 Aug. 1883.

The Three Seekers (52 couplets), *To-day*, January 1884.

Art under Plutocracy, *To-day*, February 1884.

      Do.   Do.   March   ,,

Meeting in Winter (26 couplets), *English Illustrated Magazine*, March 1884.

The Exhibition of the Royal Academy, by a rare Visitor, *To-day*, July 1884.

Letter on " The Commonweal," *Daily News*, 27 January 1885.

Letter on the Vulgarization of Oxford, *Daily News*, 20 Nov. 1885.

Letter on "The Best Hundred Books," *Pall Mall Gazette*, 2 February 1886.[1]

Letter on the League and the Federation, *Daily News*, 12 February 1886.

---

[1] This letter of a column and a fifth was reprinted in the "*Pall Mall Gazette* Extra," No. 24, on "The Best Hundred Books" (pages 10 and 11).

Letter on English Literature at the Universities, *Pall Mall Gazette*, 1 November 1886.[1]

Letter on the Civilization of our Germanic Forefathers, *Pall Mall Gazette*, 15 December 1886.

Letter on the Police and the People, *Daily News*, 17 Oct. 1887.

Do.   Do. 18 Do.

The Revival of Architecture, *Fortnightly Review*, May 1888.

The Burghers' Battle (14 quatrains), *Athenæum*, 16 June 1888.

The Revival of Handicraft, *Fortnightly Review*, November 1888.

Letter on Tapestry and Carpet-Weaving, *Times*, 2 Nov. 1888.

Letter on Mr. Shaw-Lefevre's Monumental Chapel, *Daily News*, 30 January 1889.

Westminster Abbey and its Monuments, *Nineteenth Century*, March 1889.

Letter on Monuments in Westminster Abbey, *Daily News*, 17 April 1889.

Letter on Peterborough Cathedral, *Pall Mall Gazette*, 20 September 1889.

Art and Industry in the Fourteenth Century, *Time*, Jan. 1890.

The Hall and the Wood (42 quatrains) *English Illustrated Magazine*, February 1890.

Letter on Stratford-on-Avon Church, *Times*, 15 August 1890.

The Story of the Glittering Plain, *English Illustrated Magazine*, June, July, August, and September 1890.

Letter on the Hanseatic Museum at Bergen, *Times*, 10 September 1890.

The Day of Days (poem), *Time*, November 1890.

The Socialist Ideal. I—Art (p. 152), *New Review*, January 1891.

Letter to a Liverpool gentleman on Holman Hunt's "Triumph of the Innocents," *Liverpool Daily Post*, 7 February 1891.

Letter on Westminster Abbey, *Times*, 11 February 1891.

On the Woodcuts of Gothic Books, *Times*, 25 January 1892.

Do.   Do. 28 Do.

Paper on the Woodcuts of Gothic Books (illustrated), *Journal of the Society of Arts*, 12 February 1892.

The Influence of Building Materials upon Architecture, *Century Guild Hobby Horse*, January 1892.

[1] This half-column letter reappears in the "*Pall Mall Gazette* Extra," No. 32 (page 27).

Letter on a Case before the Woolwich Magistrates, *Hammersmith Socialist Record*, April 1893.

On the Printing of Books, *Times*, 6 November 1893.

Letter on the Deeper Meaning of the Struggle (p. 169), *Daily Chronicle*, 10 November 1893.

Some Notes on the Illuminated Books of the Middle Ages, *Magazine of Art*, January 1894.

Letter on the Proposed Addition to Westminster Abbey, *Daily Chronicle*, 27 February 1894.

Letter about the Kelmscott Press Chaucer, *Daily Chronicle*, 24 July 1894.

Letter on a United Socialist Party, *Clarion*, 3 November 1894.

Letter on Peterborough Cathedral, *Times*, *Standard*, &c., 2 April 1895.

Letter on Tree-felling in Epping Forest, *Daily Chronicle*, 23 April 1895.

Letter on Tree-felling in Epping Forest (headed "Epping Forest. Mr. Morris's Report."), *Daily Chronicle*, 9 May 1895.

Letter on Royal Tombs in Westminster Abbey, *Times*, 1 June 1895.

Letter on "The Wood beyond the World," *Spectator*, 20 July 1895.

Letter on Trinity Almshouses, *Daily Chronicle*, 26 Nov. 1895.

Gossip about an Old House on the Upper Thames (p. 183), *The Quest*, November 1895.

Letter on Rouen Cathedral, *Daily Chronicle*, 12 October 1895.

Letter on Peterborough Cathedral, *Daily Chronicle*, 5 Dec. 1895.

Letter on Chichester Cathedral, *Times*, 14 December 1895.

There are a few publications, other than periodicals, containing verse or prose by Morris. In *Ancient Christmas Carols* by Edmund Sedding (London, 1860) is a poem of twelve quatrains with a chorus which is to be sung after each. It is entitled " Masters in this Hall " ; and we are told that " The English Words " were " written expressly by William Morris, Esq., B.A." It is a quaint production, sincere enough, and by no means without beauty ; but the poet did well not to challenge, by reprinting it, a comparison with his treatment of the same theme—the birth of Christ—in *The Earthly Paradise*. See " The Land East of the Sun and West of the Moon."

To the ninth edition of the *Encyclopædia Britannica* Morris conjointly with Dr. J. H. Middleton contributed the article on Mural Decoration.

The Transactions of the National Association for the Advancement of Art and its Applications contain two Addresses by Morris, one on Art and its Producers, delivered at Liverpool in 1888, the other delivered at Edinburgh in 1889, when Morris presided over the Decorative Art Section.

In the Autobiographical Notes of the Life of William Bell Scott (2 vol. 1892) there are two letters from Morris to Scott about the latter's poems.

To *Bibliographica: Papers on Books, their History and Art* (three volumes, 8vo., 1893-7), he contributed an essay " On the Artistic Qualities of the Woodcut Books of Ulm and Augsburg in the Fifteenth Century." See Vol. I. pp. 437-455.

On the 17th of March 1882 he gave evidence before the Royal Commission on Technical Education. This will be found in Vol. III. of the Second Report of the Commissioners, Presented to both Houses of Parliament by Command of Her Majesty (London, printed by Eyre and Spottiswoode, 1884). The evidence, which extends from page 150 to page 161, is excellent reading. There is a useful digest of it into two pages (cxlvi and cxlvii); but this is not such good reading. The Reports of this Commission occupy six royal 8vo. volumes (1882-4).

The following list of a few addresses, lectures, and conversations, reported in the periodical press, chronicles matters of interest more or less considerable. I have not attempted to compile a complete list of such things.

Address at Oxford on Art and Democracy, *Times*, 15 November 1883.[1]

Lecture—Useful Work *v.* Useless Toil (p. 121), *Justice*, 19 and 26 January 1884.

Lecture—Art and Socialism, *Justice*, 2 February 1884.

Lecture—Misery and the Way Out, *Justice*, 13 September 1884.

Lecture—Art and Labour, *Justice*, 27 September 1884.

A Talk with William Morris on Socialism, *Daily News*, 8 January 1885.

---

[1] This was a very brief report of the Address. In the next day's paper appeared a few lines from a correspondent stating that Morris had, on this occasion, avowed himself a Socialist.

Address at the Hammersmith Liberal Club on the Political Outlook, *Daily News*, 11 February 1886.

Representative Men at Home. Mr. William Morris at Hammersmith [including a longish report of some important utterances on his Socialism.] *Cassell's Saturday Journal*, No. 368, 18 October 1896.

Address on Early England, *Daily Chronicle*, 15 January 1894.

A Socialist Poet on Bombs and Anarchism, an Interview with William Morris, Signed "Wat Tyler," *Justice*, 27 January 1894.

Lecture—Progress of the Socialist Movement, *Justice*, 30 August 1891.

Speech at South Salford, *Justice*.

Do People Appreciate the Beautiful? A Chat with Mr. William Morris, *Cassell's Saturday Journal*, No. 628, 9 October 1895.

Address at the Funeral of Stepniak, *Times*, 30 December 1895.

Address on Disfigurement by Advertizement, *A Beautiful World*, December 1896.

There are some few reprints which I have not described because I have not seen them—and indeed have not thought it worth while to go out of my way to see them. Such are (1) *The Life and Death of Jason*, prepared and printed in 1879 solely for the use of pupils of Irvine Academy (Irvine. *Times* Office. John S. Begg); (2) the Christmas Song, printed in 1887 in the "Stream of Life Series." (Lothrop, Boston, Mass.) ; (3) an illustrated volume, published in 1888, *Atalanta's Race and other Tales*, edited with Notes by Oscar Fay Adams with the introduction by William G. Rolfe, A.M. Litt. D. (Boston, Mass., Ticknor and Co.) ; and (4) *William Morris, Poet, Artist, Socialist. A selection from his writings together with a sketch of the Man;* Edited by Francis Watts Lee (New York, Humboldt Publishing Co., 1891).

The late Francis Hueffer's Selection and Memoir form a volume worthy of record, having been done with some sort of authority. The volume is No. 2378 of the Tauchnitz Collection of British Authors,—*A Selection/ from/ the Poems/ of/ William Morris./ Edited/ With a Memoir/ by Francis Hueffer./ Copyright Edition./ Leipzig/ Bernhard Tauchnitz/ 1886./ The Right of Translation is reserved.* This may be called a Tauchnitz 8vo., since each of its 20 sheets is folded in eight, though it is more of a 16mo. shape. It consists of half-title, title, pages 5 to 20 of Memoir, pages 21 and 22 of "Contents," and pages 23 to 319 of Selections; there is a 16-page catalogue of Tauch-nitz books at the end; and the whole is done up in the usual pale buff printed wrapper.

Another selection made with authority is that given in the sixth volume of *The Poets and the Poetry of the Century*, edited by Alfred H. Miles. It was not quite easy to persuade Morris that *Sigurd the Volsung*, *The House of the Wolfings*, and *The Roots of the Mountains* ought to be represented by extracts; but when I had done my biographical sketch, he waived his objections; and on looking at the book again I cannot but think he did well. The passage taken from *Sigurd* is not hurt by excision; while *The Tale of the Hauberk*, from *The Wolfings*, and the two songs from *The Roots of the Mountains*, are per-fectly detachable. The first edition of this volume came out in April 1891; and a second (revised) was published in May 1896. The title-page of the first edition, which is undated, reads—*The/ Poets/ and the/ Poetry/ of the/ Century/ William Morris/ to/ Robert Buchanan/ Edited by/ Alfred H. Miles/ Hutchinson & Co./ 25, Paternoster Square, London;* and that of the second is only changed by the alteration of the address to "34, Paternoster Row" and the addition of the date "1896." Both books alike consist of half-title, title, pages iii to xii of preface and "index," a second half-title, and 596 pages of text.

SUMMARY LIST

OF THE

Books Issued from the Kelmscott Press

WITH THE DATES ON WHICH THEY WERE FINISHED AND
THE PAGES OF THE PRESENT VOLUME AT WHICH
FURTHER PARTICULARS OF THEM MAY BE
FOUND.

The Story of the Glittering Plain, 1st edition, 4 April 1891, pp. 14, 156.

Poems by the Way, 24 September 1891, pp. 15, 158.

The Love Lyrics and Songs of Proteus by Wilfrid Scawen Blunt with the Love Sonnets of Proteus by the same Author now reprinted in their full text with many Sonnets omitted from the earlier Editions, 26 January 1892, p. 160.

The Nature of Gothic by Ruskin, colophon undated, preface dated 15 February 1892, p. 163.

The Defence of Guenevere &c., 2 April 1892, p. 38.

A Dream of John Ball &c., 13 May 1892, p. 139.

The Golden Legend of Master William Caxton (3 vol. 4to.), 12 September 1892, p. 164.

The Recuyell of the Historyes of Troye (2 vol. 4to.), 14 October 1892, p. 164.

Biblia Innocentium by J. W. Mackail, 22 October 1892, p. 164.

News from Nowhere, 22 November 1892, p. 150.

The History of Reynard the Foxe, 15 December 1892, p. 164.

The Poems of William Shakespeare, 17 January 1893, p. 165.

The Order of Chivalry &c., 24 February 1893, p. 165.

The Life of Cardinal Wolsey by George Cavendish, 30 March 1893, p. 166.

The History of Godfrey of Boloyne, 27 April 1893, p. 166.

Utopia by Sir Thomas More, 4 August 1893, p. 167.

Maud a Monodrama by Alfred Lord Tennyson, 11 August 1893, p. 168.

Sidonia the Sorceress, translated from Meinhold by Lady Wilde, 15 September 1893, p. 168.

Gothic Architecture, a Lecture by Morris, Autumn 1893, p. 171.

Ballads and Narrative Poems by D. G. Rossetti, 14 October 1893, p. 172.

The Tale of King Florus and the Fair Jehane, 16 December 1893, p. 172.

The Story of the Glittering Plain, with 23 Pictures by Walter Crane, 13 January 1894, p. 157.

Sonnets and Lyrical Poems by D. G. Rossetti, 20 February 1894, p. 172.

The Poems of John Keats [a Selection], edited by F. S. Ellis, 7 March 1894, p. 172.

Of the Friendship of Amis and Amile, 13 March 1894, p. 172.

Atalanta in Calydon, a Tragedy made by Algernon Charles Swinburne, 4 May 1894, p. 175.

The Wood beyond the World, 30 May 1894, pp. 15, 177.

The Tale of the Emperor Coustans &c., 30 August 1894, p. 176.

The Book of Wisdom and Lies translated by Oliver Wardrop, 29 September 1894, p. 181.

Psalmi Penitentiales, 15 November 1894, p. 181.

Epistola de Contemptu Mundi di Frate Hieronymo [Savonarola] da Ferrara, [edited by Charles Fairfax Murray from an autograph manuscript with a portrait of Savonarola designed by the editor and engraved by William H. Hooper,] 30 November 1894, p. 181.

The Tale of Beowulf, 10 January 1895, pp. 15,181..

Syr Percivelle of Gales, 16 February 1895, p. 182.

The Life and Death of Jason, with two woodcuts after Sir E. Burne-Jones, 25 May 1895, p. 50.

The Story of Child Christopher and Goldiliud the Fair, 25 July 1895, pp. 16, 182.

The Poetical Works of Percy Bysshe Shelley, edited by F. G. Ellis, 21 August 1895, pp. 181, 182, 183.

Hand and Soul, by D. G. Rossetti, 24 October 1895, p. 183.

Poems chosen out of the Works of Robert Herrick, edited by F. S. Ellis, 21 November 1895, p. 183.

Poems chosen out of the Works of Samuel Taylor Coleridge, edited by F. S. Ellis, 5 February 1896, p. 184.

The Well at the World's End, 2 March 1896, pp. 16, 184, 187-8.

The Works of Geoffrey Chaucer, edited by F. S. Ellis, with 86 pictures by Sir E. Burne-Jones, 8 May 1896, pp. 17, 189.

Laudes Beatae Mariae Virginis : Poems "taken from a Psalter written by an English scribe, most likely in one of the Midland counties, early in the 13th century," [printed in black, red, and blue], 7 July 1896, p. 189.

The Floure and the Leafe &c., edited by F. S. Ellis, 21 August 1896, p. 189.

The Earthly Paradise, 8 volumes, Vol. i., 7 May 1896. Vol. viii., 10 June 1897, pp. 72-5.

The Shepheardes Calendar, 14 October 1896, p. 189.

The Water of the Wondrous Isles, 1 April 1897, p. 190.[1]

[1] The remaining five books named in this list had not been delivered when the present volume was "passed for press."

Sire Degravauut, an Ancient English Metrical Romance with woodcut after Sir E. Burne-Jones.

Sire Isumbras [companion volume to Sire Degravaunt], with woodcut after Sir E. Burne-Jones.

Sigurd the Volsung and the Fall of the Niblungs, small folio, with two woodcuts after Sir E. Burne-Jones and new borders by Morris, p. 89.

The Sundering Flood, Morris's last Romance, 8vo., to be bound in half-holland, pp. 16, 191.

Love is Enough, quarto, Troy type, in black, red, and blue, with a woodcut after Sir E. Burne-Jones, p. 191.

KELMSCOTT PRESS MISCELLANEA.

Two Specimen Pages of Froissart's Works, with the special armorial border and ornaments designed for this book by William Morris. Folio, printed on vellum [no paper copies], issued to subscribers in the ordinary way.

Incomplete sheets of the Froissart. 32 copies printed at the Kelmscott Press on Dec. 24, 1896, before the distribution of the type. Not for sale [four folio sheets, with 1 heraldic design by Morris].

Incomplete sheet of Sigurd the Volsung. 32 copies printed at the Kelmscott Press on Jan. 11, 1897, before the distribution of the type. Not for sale [folio sheet with border and two ornamental letters by Morris], p. 89.

Laudes Beatae Mariae Virginis : a single leaf bearing a note dated 28th of December 1896, to the effect that the Poems mentioned above were printed in 1579 and ascribed to Stephen Langton.

Vitas Patrum : Prospectus, Order form and specimen page of a projected reprint of St. Jerome's Lives of the Fathers of the Desert, as translated by Caxton and printed by Wynken de Worde. This was to have been edited by F. S. Ellis, and printed in the golden type uniformly with the Golden Legend. The project was abandoned for want of subscribers.

Mr. William Morris's Productions of the Kelmscott Press : a four-page circular issued by Mr. Quaritch in February 1893. The circular, which contains an "appreciation" by Morris of Caxton's "Recuyell of the Histories of Troye," was not printed at the Kelmscott Press; but it is scarcely complete without an item which was " to be had on application,"—to-wit, "The full Colophon-title and Caxton's preface, as they appear in the Morris edition," —a four-page specimen of the noble quarto, with Morris's colophon set immediately under Caxton's " prologe."

Prospectus of " Sidonia the Sorceress," 1894, p. 168.

Kelmscott Press Edition of Chaucer's Works. A letter signed " William Morris " and dated 14 November 1894, announcing that there will be over 70 instead of 60 pictures by Sir E. Burne-Jones, and 425 instead of 325 copies of the book.

London County Council. Technical Education Board. Two ornamentally-bordered forms of certificate, (1) as to the granting of junior county scholarships, (2) as to attendance at a school of domestic economy. Both have blanks for details to be filled in in manuscript, and spaces for signatures.

Form of invitation issued by the Hammersmith Socialist Society to an entertainment at Kelmscott House on the 30th of January 1892. Two oblong leaves ·(one blank) $4\frac{1}{2} \times 3$ inches.

An American Memorial to Keats. Announcement of intention to meet at Hampstead Parish Church and unveil the bust of Keats by Miss Anne Whitney of Boston, Mass.

An Address " To Sir Lowthian Bell, Baronet, F.R.S., D.C.L., &c., &c., the Founder of the Firm of Bell Brothers in the year 1844 " (4 leaves 8vo.).

In Memory of Thomas Sadler, Ph.D. 15 lines of Golden type capitals, set up and printed off as a pattern to be enlarged at 449 Oxford Street, for a mural inscription.

Paper of Membership for the Ancoats Brotherhood, 1894-5, four pages, namely the Frontispiece of the Kelmscott *John Ball*, and three pages of extracts from Tennyson and Ruskin.

Specimen of the Golden Type for the Devinne Press, written by Morris and printed on a single leaf. It starts with an ornamental T, two inches square, initial to the words— " The Kelmscott Press began work in Hammersmith in February 1891."

Specimen page of the three Kelmscott types for Mr. E. F. Strange's *Alphabets* (both large and small paper) published by Messrs. George Bell and Sons in their " *Ex Libris* Series " in 1895.

The Deaconess Institution for the Diocese of Rochester, 83 North Side, Clapham Common. Associates' Card. A prayer set in the Troy type within an ornamental border and printed on a card measuring 6¼ × 5 inches, folded in two, with the above heading and some Rules printed on the new recto and a Bible text on the verso,—this outside printing in the Chaucer type.

The catalogues, lists, and mere business announcements of the Press, which are numerous and varied, I have not thought it necessary to mention in detail.

THE END.

BILLING AND SONS, PRINTERS, GUILDFORD.